T0327948

# FRANCHISE

# FRANCHISE

## Trusting God First...Then Yourself

Seth Coleman

ELM HILL

A Division of
HarperCollins Christian Publishing

www.elmhillbooks.com

© 2020 Seth Coleman

# Franchise

### Trusting God First…Then Yourself

All rights reserved. No portion of this book may be reproduced, stored in a retrieval system, or transmitted in any form or by any means—electronic, mechanical, photocopy, recording, scanning, or other—except for brief quotations in critical reviews or articles, without the prior written permission of the publisher.

Published in Nashville, Tennessee, by Elm Hill, an imprint of Thomas Nelson. Elm Hill and Thomas Nelson are registered trademarks of HarperCollins Christian Publishing, Inc.

Elm Hill titles may be purchased in bulk for educational, business, fund-raising, or sales promotional use. For information, please e-mail SpecialMarkets@ ThomasNelson.com.

Publisher's Note: This novel is a work of fiction. Names, characters, places, and incidents are either products of the author's imagination or used fictitiously. All characters are fictional, and any similarity to people living or dead is purely coincidental.

All Scripture quotations are taken from the King James Version. Public domain.

### Library of Congress Cataloging-in-Publication Data

Library of Congress Control Number: 2019915667

ISBN 978-1-400329250 (Paperback)
ISBN 978-1-400329267 (Hardbound)
ISBN 978-1-400329274 (eBook)

# DEDICATION

The story you are about to read is fiction with a twist. During my career in public relations and marketing, I was blessed to work for a couple very similar to Will and Winnie who you will read about in my story. Their names were Bill and Bonnie LeVine, and I was fortunate to work with them soon out of college. They were pioneers in American franchising that were loved and admired by franchise owners, their employees, and those within the franchising industry. I learned business integrity from them, and being a young man, I thought of them as a second set of parents. During those years, I secretly wanted to be an author and every interesting thing that happened became the basis for a novel. In 1994, the International Franchise Association created the Bonnie LeVine Award in recognition of her outstanding accomplishments in franchising and of her status as a role model for women in the franchise community. And for those who knew Bonnie … let's remember her absolutely unforgettable laugh!

So, here it is, based on some experiences and some facts intertwined with an active imagination.

# Franchise Characters

*Bible references are included as a footnote on the appropriate page in the*
*King James version - KJV*

## POP's Office Supply Corporate

Greg Martinez - National Sales Manager

Daniel Davidson - Regional Marketing Manager

Will LaTrove - former President of POP's

Winnie LaTrove - wife of Will and former PR Director

Tim Morrison - New President*

Mack Costello - VP Marketing*
- Wife: Carole
- Daughter: Rachael

Joe Farrow - Director of Operation

Susan Heart - Gossip, works in mail room

Ray Shaman - New Vice President of Sales*

John - Daniel's team member

Stephen - Daniel's team member

Susan - Daniel's team member

Mari Lee - Director of IT at POP's

## Balaam Basor Investments

Leland Belial (Lee)

Melinda Carlson

Tim Morrison - New President*

Mack Costello - VP Marketing

Joe Farrow - VP - Director of Operations

Ray Shaman - New Vice President of Sales*

Haman Estes - Vice President of Finance

## On the Plane to Rome

Stefan - Passenger #1

Lance - Passenger #2

Jim - Works for Comfort Industries Associated. (CIA)

Joe - Sat next to Jim on plane

## FBI

Doug Hensley - Special Agent, meets plane from Rome

## Comfortable Industries Associated

Jim - works for CIA
Joe - Man in seat on plane to Rome

## POP's Franchise Owners

Dottie Daye - Texas
Lance Schiffold - Michigan
Jerry Jones - New York
Sam Salerno - Ill
Sloan Dickinson - Franchise owner, Paramus, NJ
Darryl - Brother to Sloan Dickinson, works on Wall Street,

## Important Business Related

GFI - Global Franchise Society
POP's Franchise Owners Association
FTC - Federal Trade Commission
Jim Foley - BBI contact at Federal Trade commission (FTC)

## 666

Lucifer / Satan
Havoc / demon #1
Ruination / demon #2
Furor / demon #3

## 777

Melchior Archangel: (pronounced Mell-shy-or)
Haszik Guardian Angel: humility, faith, and obedience were his great character elements

## Others

Dana - Daniel's fiancee
Tad - Dana's son
Curt Wisely - insurance adjuster
Uncle Sprandy and Beulah
American Embassy Rome - John
Daniel's fake ID - Robert Banks
Greg's fake ID - Harry Jones
Darryl Dickinson, brother to Sloan, stock trader on Wall Street
Jill - Daniel's sister
Troy - Jill's oldest son
Clay - Jill's youngest son
Sprandy and Beulah - Daniel's aunt and uncle
American Embassy Rome - John
Hal - Jill's ex husband
Frances - Lady on school bus at airport
Chuck and Sandy - helped Daniel and Greg get back to Los Angeles on their private plane

# PROLOGUE

Thunder rumbled and rolled through the sky high above Southern California, followed seconds later by flashes of lightning traveling from one cloud to another, illuminating the heavens for a millisecond. From Malibu, the view was awe inspiring. Two angels stood on the beach beside each other, their attention shifting as they watched the heavenly display. They gazed toward the black expanse of the Pacific and simultaneously bowed as a short burst of light penetrated the night, silhouetting a tiny ship traveling to Asia against the horizon. An instant later, following a second and more intense burst of radiance, the vast sea was again cloaked in an absence of light. The messengers now turned inland as they quietly rose to a higher vantage point where they could peer over the coastal mountains. This time the flash of light cracked just above their heads, brightening all of Topanga Canyon for a fleeting instant, and startling the drivers traveling on the Coastal Highway below.

Having now risen high above the myriad of lights lining the Los Angeles Basin, the emissaries focused on their objective. Silently, they floated down the stiffening air currents toward the six-story office building in Calabasas.

Large drops of rain began to land onto the structure and surrounding area. Blown by the storm, they slammed against the windows of the building with increasing intensity. Fortunately, there was not any one inside to hear. The two looked upward toward the cirrus clouds high above the earth and then to the puffy cumulus ones intensifying below. Instantly, the billows transformed to darker shades of gray. The leading spirit blew softly and a violent wind began falling from on high, gaining speed as it headed toward the ground. The monsoon force winds were positioned and aimed perfectly above their target. Confidently, the second angel raised one arm toward his home, offering praise to his creator and acknowledging that, although he did not know the reason, the outcome would be for His glory.

Then suddenly, in the midst of the deluge, a well-formed crack of lightning found its way to the air conditioner on the top of the office building. Sparks flew in all directions, cascading over the edges and plummeting toward the ground by the driven wind. The gale concentrated its power on the roof until it gave way. Designed to withstand an earthquake, the sturdy edifice was no match for an Act of God. Through two floors, the man-made machinery plummeted, shattering glass and crushing all in its path until the edges of mangled metal penetrated the office of its president.

# CHAPTER 1

Six Months Before Franchise Conclave
Boardroom Balaam Basor Investments
Willis Tower
Chicago, Illinois, USA

The **Willis Tower**, still referred to by many as the **Sears Tower**, is Chicago's premier office address and currently its most popular tourist destination, attracting more than one million people per year to its observation decks. When it was built in 1973, it was the tallest building in the country at 1,450 feet, and still remains the building with the most floors, 110—five more than **One World Trade Center** in New York, which holds the title for being the tallest building in the United States at 1,776 feet.

The offices of **Balaam Basor Investments**, located in the penthouse, commands an impressive view across Lake Michigan to the neighboring states of Indiana, Michigan, and Wisconsin. But there is a price to pay for the breathtaking panorama. When gusts are roaring in Chicago, known as the Windy City, the swaying sends many new employees running for the bathroom until their stomachs eventually adjust to the occasionally frightening motion.

To enhance their guests' experience, the entrance from the elevator opens to a central lobby, bedecked with marble floors, statues of Greek gods, and a bronze sculpture of the earth that dominates the space, strategically placed in the midst of a giant two-story window which framed the extraordinary landscape behind it. Then, as a bit of overstatement, clients and visitors could walk on the famous retractable glass-bottomed balcony, one of only two in the building, that was situated directly behind it and extended four feet out from the side of the building, when the wind was not too strong. First-time clients were invariably astonished at the sensation of hovering far above Wacker Drive with the illusion of nothing below their feet. Those brave enough would read words etched in the transparency beneath, only visible by standing directly on top of them.

## Welcome to Balaam Basor Investments.
## Join Us in Our Vision
## To Possess Our Share of the World.

Melinda, along with the other six people in the boardroom that day, had seen the sight many times. Each of them was personally selected for this elite and secret division of the company. She smiled casually as she entered and carefully chose the comfortable low-back seat at the center of the massive redwood table. She positioned herself directly across from the entrance, with her back against another massive window. Flawlessly dressed with flowing reddish-brown hair, she commanded a presence of professionalism. She surveyed her associates with sincere admiration, loving the way each of the men were impeccably dressed and seemed to exude their own personal air of affluence. Like herself, each was experienced in hostile takeovers. This group alone had a combined total of almost one hundred years' experience in knowing how to collapse companies from within.

Leland Belial, or Lee to those closest to him, was there to personally greet his veteran team of professionals. Tapping his pen rapidly on his water glass, he called the meeting to order.

"As **Chief Executive Officer**, I want to welcome all of you once again to **BBI** headquarters to discuss your newest assignment. As you know, we have recently acquired a significant share of stock and are in final negotiations for the leverage buyout of **POP's Office Supply Franchise**. We have already begun our infiltration and expect final takeover in a few months. Since this is our first endeavor at a franchise, it will be a new experience for all of us, but one no harder than the others. In fact, we are expecting that it will, in the long run, work in our favor.

"Melinda, you are already working for them. How do you like your new job as Executive Secretary to the President?"

"Absolutely loving it!" Melinda spoke clearly and confidently. An attractive thirty-two-year-old, she was the newest to the team with only eleven years' experience. "I like Los Angeles, and as far as I can tell, they do not have a clue what is heading their way."

"Good. How about Will LaTrove? I understand that he is revered by the franchise owners."

"True," she said, nodding as she answered, "they trust him and see him as a genuinely good man who looks out for their best interests, so I would completely agree with that."

"Do you think he suspects you?"

"No, not at all. I believe I have already gained his trust. In fact, he invited me to lunch, along with his wife, a few weeks ago. Nice couple." She added, "One thing I can tell you is that no one is happy they are retiring. It is the main topic of conversation right now."

"Good, glad to hear it. I have been expecting both the owners and the employees to be unhappy. That's why the timing works out so well for us."

Now addressing the rest of the group who had been listening intently, Belial said, "Melinda started as his secretary a few months ago and is our eyes and ears until Tim arrives next month as the new President." He smiled at Melinda.

"About that timing, Lee ..." Tim Morrison interrupted. "I just read in today's *Wall Street Journal* that LaTrove has already selected his replacement but has been keeping it under wraps. According to the report, the new president is to start in three weeks."

"Very well aware of that. Tim and I have it under control," Belial said reassuringly with a devilish grin. "One of the presidents of our top subsidiary holdings is being fired as we speak to make a place for him. The position will be offered to LaTrove's new Golden Boy at a salary he will not be able to refuse. That will leave you, his second choice, to fill the now open spot for the new President of the franchise."

"It will only work if he accepts the position. Do you think he will take it?" Joe Farrow asked.

"Yes. We are sure of it. We also have arranged a rather substantial loss in one of his personal investments, so I think he will be in the market for the job paying the highest salary. And of course, if that isn't enough, there are other ways of preventing him from showing up to work. You will get the job, Tim. Don't worry about it."

"What is your take on how the stock market will react to the change?" asked Ray Shaman, soon to be the newest member of POP's sales staff as Vice President of Sales.

"We are expecting the stock prices to remain on a steady incline throughout the transition," Ray answered. "Much of the stock, aside from ours, is owned by the franchise owners themselves, and like Melinda said, they trust Will in choosing the right person to take over the reins of the company. We don't expect them to start falling until the third quarter. That is, of course, if all works out as planned."

"I met with Greg Martinez, Senior Sales Manager, a few weeks ago," Ray chimed in, "and after he *reviewed my references.*" He paused for a moment, glancing at the rest of the group who joined him in a knowing smile, then continued, "I start work next week as the newest member of the senior staff and his brand-new boss."

"Congratulations on your new job, Ray," Melinda said mischievously. "I look forward to meeting you for the first time when you begin. Perhaps we can even have lunch some time."

"That's a good idea, Melinda," Belial said. "In fact, I think it might be a better idea if you two start a relationship. It will give the both of you a chance to get together to compare notes without being suspected."

"Great," Melinda said, agreeing as she looked across the large conference room table at the handsome new salesman.

"I think I can handle that," Ray said, giving her a wink.

"That reminds me, Ray," Belial said, raising his finger in the air remembering he had some information to pass along to him. "My nephew and his wife will be interviewing at Corporate in a few weeks and want to open a location in Pennsylvania. Since you are from Pittsburgh, it should be easy to convince him to give the prospects to you. It will not be a secret they are related to me, as it will appear a good-faith move on my part to have members of my own family involved. Following the two of them, I will be sending you a few other prospects to be placed in each of the regions here in the USA. Four altogether, plus another two in Europe and one each in Japan and Hong Kong, but I do not have a line on who they will be yet."

"Thanks, I like a shoo-in." Ray smiled.

Joe Farrow, future Executive Vice President of Operations, offered a few more of the details. "These owners will be keeping their ears to the ground, updating us on the franchise owner pulse. We expect each of you will go out of your way to become associated with them in some way."

"I am not sure all of you are aware of this," Tim Morrison added, "but **BBI** has people retained in strategic places within the franchising industry, including **FSI**. For those of you not familiar with the acronym, get used to the initials as you will hear it a lot. It stands for **Franchise Society International**, and offers the most visible information available to perspective franchise owners. This will guarantee us good press coverage with regard to the takeover and remove any doubt that **POP's** will be heralded as a good investment. A fact we can thank Will for. He has a stellar reputation within the industry which will allow our man to get pretty much what he wants from his bosses. And of course, Jim, who most of you know and have dealt with previously, is in the **Federal Trade Commission**. Melinda, I think you are the only one here who has not met him, therefore you do not know his role. The **FTC** is an independent government agency which promotes consumer protection. Any allegations of fraud would first be reported to them."

"You have people everywhere," Melinda said, impressed.

"Not everywhere," interjected Belial. "But I can take pride in saying that **BBI** has them everywhere it is important." He hesitated getting back to his agenda. "Melinda, I want to turn to you for a moment. I would like an evaluation of the movers and shakers at the company, both employees and franchise owners."

"Sure, I think you are asking who I think we need to be wary of, am I right?"

"You're right on the money!" Belial added, addressing the rest of the group, "I like this girl."

Melinda flipped open her iPad and entered her password, allowing her to view her private notes. "At this point, there are only four names on my list, three employees and one franchise owner. I am sure the list will grow, but right now this is what I have. I will add more as I become aware of them, but for the moment, these are the ones I suggest we watch from the get-go.

"Number one is Daniel Davison. Oh, my goodness… what a Mary Poppins. Have you guys ever seen the reruns of *Leave It to Beaver*? He is like Eddie Haskell with a twist. That twist being he is not only polite, but appears to be sincere in his caring for the needs of the franchise owners. He is also sharp as a tack and very protective of the LaTroves. Will he be sharp enough to figure out what is going on? I am not sure."

"Mary Poppins?" Belial asked. "Are you saying he's gay?"

"Not sure. He doesn't appear that way to me at all. It was just something one of the secretaries said and there may not be anything to it. Could have been sour grapes. I think she had the hots for him and he was definitely not interested. I understand he is engaged to a teacher from Los Angeles, although he lives in Florida and does seem to have eyes for Viviana, our travel specialist, but then everyone has eyes for her, even me." She laughed. "But I have heard a few rumors. So, in answer to your question, I will get back to you on that one."

"Please do. Information like that might be helpful to us at some point … you can never tell."

"How do you mean, if you don't mind me asking?"

"I don't mind at all." Belial continued as if describing a normal way of doing business: "Sometimes it is necessary to get information from people in unorthodox ways; gaining their trust through a relationship is the easiest, and sometimes pillow talk is the least suspicious." He paused a moment, thinking. "At times we have used prostitutes, but longer-term relationships are preferable. Of course, either way we would need to know gender attractions to make it work. In fact, now that you mentioned it, Melinda, it might be a good idea for you to forgo a relationship with Ray and concentrate on Daniel. What do you think?"

"Done!"

"Good girl. Anything else we should know about him?"

"Yes, he is in the field most of the time consulting with franchise owners as he is a Regional Manager in the Southern States, although he was originally in their advertising department a number of years ago." She looked up from her notes. "At one point, he left **POP's** for a stint with **McDonald's**, then returned several years later. That's to say he has been around for a while." She paged through her notes while speaking. "I reviewed his employee records, and several of the evaluations from past supervisors state that the franchise owners 'love him.' One reference letter from Human Resources refers to him as an outstanding employee. He spends little time at the LA office, so it may take a while to get a meaningful relationship going with him to really find out all he knows, but right now …" she paused, considering her words, "I doubt he is in the loop that involves us, other than what he hears from the franchise owners in the field and friends at corporate. He could be easy or a serious problem, I'm not sure which. We will just have to wait and see. But leave it to me, I'll find out.

"Next is Greg Martinez, Senior Sales Manager. He is both smart, sharp and who will be working with Ray starting next week. He and Daniel are close friends and I am guessing what one knows, the other does as well. There is no question as to his sexual identity … he's a real Romeo. Nice guy, too. I like him."

"Says the girl that calls him a Romeo," Ray teased.

"Watch it, buddy. Word has it that you're a bit of a lady *killer* yourself," she teased back, "if you get my drift." She snickered. "In fact, didn't I hear something about that recently?"

"That's enough, Melinda," Belial said calmly, his voice commanding. "Those are subjects that are never discussed. Am I clear?"

"Yes, sir." Waiting until the group finished suppressing their laughter she continued. "As far as franchise owners, it would be Dottie Day from Dallas that would be my biggest concern. She is the Vice President of **POP's** Franchise Owners Association and like another Will LaTrove, well loved by all. It makes me want to puke. Anyway, at this point she is the one who concerns me the most, so keep your eye on her. She has Will's ear, as well as Daniel's and Greg's.

"Lastly, if you want to spread gossip that will go like wildfire throughout the company, get to know Susan Hart. She is my nomination for **POP's** resident gossipmonger. She works in the mail room and is into everyone's business. It doesn't matter to her if they are corporate employees or franchise owners; if it is a juicy tidbit, she's onto it … a good one to keep in your rumor mill loop. But be careful. She comes across like a ding bat, but I think she has some latent intelligence beneath that exterior."

"Okay then," said Belial, indicating that the meeting was nearing its end. "Tim, do you have anything to add?"

"Only this, Melinda, Ray … when we are at POP's, remember we do not have any relationship other than employee and boss and you must keep it that way. Mack and Joe and I will have more interaction, but we must keep it only professional as well. If any of you have information to convey, send it from your secured line to **BBI** and they will get it to me. Under no circumstances are you to contact me directly at work or even at my home unless it is strictly within your job description at **POP's**. If Mr. Belial thinks it necessary to get together, he will make the arrangements." Tim smiled warmly and nodded to the group. "Okay, you are all professionals, let's get to work, make some money and bring this company down."

# Chapter 2

Three Months Before Franchise Conclave
POP's Corporate Headquarters
Calabasas, California

"Hey, handsome, how are you doing? Glad you stopped by. Are you here to see Will or is it an excuse to see me?" she teased.

"Not too bad, Melinda. Yes, it is always a pleasure to see you, and another yes; is he in?" Daniel said, smiling.

"Yes and no. He is in, but now is not a good time."

"Why, what's up?" Daniel asked, grinning.

"He's meeting with Tim and one of the new investors and it doesn't sound like it is going too well so far."

"I'm sorry to hear …" Daniel's voice trailed off at the sound of loud voices coming from Will's former office. He was surprised to hear Will so outraged.

"You are not going to take my company and turn it into …"

"Stop it." Daniel heard Tim interrupting Will, and then saying in a firm steady voice, "**BBI** has the controlling interest in **POP's**. From now on they make all policy and decisions. I understand how hard this must be for you, but you might as well get used to it. You have turned the reins over to me. Now you are going to have to trust me to do the best for the company and the franchise owners. **BBI** expects me to increase sales and improve stock prices. That is my objective and what I was hired to do." He lied convincingly.

"I understand about stock prices ..." Daniel could hear something slamming on the desk, guessing it was Will's fist. "But what you are doing will not work with franchise owners who are used to having influence on those decisions. I have taught the concept of slow and steady growth to every employee I have ever had. The franchise owner has always come first. We took care of them; they succeeded; and we all made money. What you are doing will ruin the company."

Daniel heard a third person begin to speak. He strained intently to hear the unfamiliar voice. It was much lower, very controlled, and sent a shiver down his spine. "That is outdated thinking, Will. It is not going to fly with **BBI**. You have to stop with the old ways of thinking and realize that you have no say in decisions going forward."

There was a pause for a few seconds, then Tim spoke. "That is why our stockholders are investing in us."

"You are nothing more than a stooge for **BBI**. They are not the ones who hired you; I am." Daniel could hear Will's voice quaver.

"I am truly sorry you feel that way, Will, but I am sure you can understand my hands are tied. I plan to look out for the franchise owners just like you did. Give me some time to prove it to you and you'll see."

"I doubt it!" Will snapped with the sound of disgust.

Daniel watched as the office door opened so hard it slammed against its stop. Without saying a word, Will stormed past him, arriving at the elevator just in time to catch the doors closing, and then he was gone.

"Well, Melinda, there's something I've never seen before," Daniel said, leaning against the half wall close to her desk.

"I'm afraid that is not the first time I have heard arguing from in there. In fact, I think if Will still had control of the company, he would have fired Tim."

"Really?" Daniel said, truly surprised.

"Yes, I think he is having a hard time letting go. I really feel for him

… I don't blame him." She added, "He grew a fantastic company. Then to have it pulled out right from under him must be hard."

"Wow … well, that was really something," he said, leaning forward and placing his hand on her desk while speaking softly. "It is going to take my brain a while to process what I just heard."

"Well, don't strain it too hard, Daniel," she said encouragingly. "Tim is really doing a great job. I field all his calls from the owners and they seem to really like him. When Will finally lets go, I think he will be able to see it. It's just going to take some time." She reached over and placed her hand on top of his in a provocative gesture. "I understand the two of you are friends. Maybe it would be a good idea to say a few words to him. Help him work it all out."

"Me," Daniel said nostalgically, "friends? He is more like a father to me." Daniel smiled. "Did you ever try to tell your father what to do?"

"Point well taken," she said, laughing, and adding pleasantly, "I'm glad you are in town. Maybe we will have some time to grab dinner while you are here?" She made the suggestion coyly.

"I doubt dinner, but perhaps lunch. I'll try to work it in," Daniel said, looking at his watch while walking to the elevator backwards.

"Good, I'll look forward to it," she said nonchalantly, rearranging some papers on her desk, then reaching for the phone.

"Later. My guys are waiting for me in Operations and I'm late." He disappeared into the elevator and then stuck his hand out of the door and waved to her.

Melinda smiled, satisfied with herself. *What a jerk,* she thought.

Daniel stopped to greet a few people on his way to the Operations center. By the time he walked in, Mack was already talking to his team.

"Sorry, I am late. What did I miss?" he said, addressing Mack. "Hi, John, Stephan, Susan." He nodded and give them a warm smile.

"I was getting to know your team," Mack responded. "Now that you are all here, I just wanted you to know we do not foresee any marketing changes at this time. You guys are doing an outstanding job. Comments from the franchise owners reflect that. I have reviewed your site surveys, grand opening reports, first-year follow-ups, and the owners are happy."

"We are glad to hear that, Mack. On that note, I thought you might like some good news we have to share with you."

"Good news? I can't wait to hear it. What have you guys been up to?"

Daniel grinned at his team before starting. "We had a coordinator meeting in Dallas a few weeks ago and while we were there, I invited a representative from the **United States Postal Service** to join us. I didn't mention it to you earlier because it was just an idea and a long shot at best, but here is the plan.

"I called their headquarters in Washington, D.C., to ask them if they would consider placing a satellite **USPS** station in our stores. It would be a completely self-contained unit with account-based billing, a little larger than the standard **UPS/FedEx** drop boxes, but large enough to weigh packages, electronically charge postage and ship. This would create new foot traffic, ultimately generating additional revenue into **POP's**." Daniel looked for a reaction from Mack. Seeing none, he continued, "Frankly, I was surprised when they called back. The bottom line is that they are willing to do a test in downtown Dallas. I did not say anything to our owners yet as we wanted to get your approval before proceeding."

"Interesting thought, you guys. I am glad to see your initiative." Mack hesitated, clearly not quite knowing how to continue. "However, I am not positive it fits into our future marketing strategy."

"Not a fit, Mack?" Daniel looked at his team. The shocked expressions on their faces matched his own. "Mack, this will give every local business an added incentive to visit our locations. It is an incredible opportunity to create new business flow into the stores for our owners. Mack …" Daniel searched for the right words to convince his new boss. "This is a win-win situation if I ever saw one. There is no downside, everyone wins! I don't understand what your concern would be."

"Guys, we have a global marketing strategy." He paused, carefully thinking how to answer. "I am not sure it is a good fit. That is all," he said flatly. "But I will run it past Tim to see what he has to say." Mack stood up to leave, then added, "Really good work. I want to encourage you all to keep coming up with these ideas. I will let you know what the senior staff has to say, but I wouldn't get your hopes up. It would not be a good idea to mention it to the franchise owners at this point." He nodded and walked out the door.

"Daniel, you got a second?"

"Sure." Daniel moved outside the door to speak to him privately.

"I see you planned to stay in California this weekend, and Carole and I would like to invite you over for a barbecue Saturday if you can make it."

"I was planning on spending the time with Dana."

"No problem. Please bring her along. We would love to meet her."

"Okay, I'm sure she would like that, too. Thanks for inviting us."

"Great, it's all settled. We will see you then. Stop by and see Melinda before you go and she will give you the directions."

"Sure. Thanks."

As Daniel returned to the meeting, all three of the coordinators started talking at the same time.

"Wait," he said, raising his hand. "I am just as surprised as you are that he wasn't ecstatic about the idea, but there is a bright side. If they do not approve this idea, then they must have something really special up their sleeve for the owners. Let's just wait and see. Now let's go on and discuss your problem locations. Stephan, you first …"

# CHAPTER 3

Home of Mack Costello
POP's Director of Marketing
Malibu, California
11 Miles from Calabasas

"I love the drive through Malibu," Dana said lovingly, while reaching over and placing her hand on Daniel's leg. "I wish we had more days like this to spend together."

"Once we're married, we will have years for times like this," Daniel said. "I'm looking forward to it, too." Daniel exhaled with a smile as he looked out over the coastline toward Oxnard. "Dana, this is such an incredibly beautiful area." He said it as if he wanted to holler it to anyone who would listen. "The air is absolutely crystal clear, especially after that thunderstorm last night." He turned off the air conditioning and opened both of the windows. "Smell that unpolluted ocean air," he said while taking a deep breath. "It is a wonderful day to be in LA!" He then yelled out the window: "HELLO, LA!… I WANT TO COME HOME!"

Dana laughed. "That's a nice thought, Daniel, but it won't happen with you running all over the country every week visiting franchise owners."

"Well, hopefully that will be changing. I think that may be why Mack invited us to his home for a barbecue. He knows we are getting married and I think he wants to meet you, probably to see if you are good enough to present to the owners," he said mischievously.

"You're asking for it," she said, teasing back and giving him a pinch on the leg.

"OUCH," he said, squirming a bit. "That hurt!"

"Sorry."

"You know, I really do think he has a reason for inviting us. He may be thinking about bringing me back to work at corporate."

"Really, Daniel, that would be great," she said excitedly. "Why didn't you tell me this sooner? I have been wrestling with the idea of leaving my family and job to move to Florida."

"I know, I could tell. I didn't want to say anything to get your hopes up, and it still may not work out, but now I think there is a good possibility."

"Why, what changed?"

Daniel took a breath and exhaled. "At this point, it is purely speculation, but Mack came to one of our regional coordinator meetings when I was here at corporate this past week. He wanted to introduce himself to me and the guys." Then he smiled and added, "He said that the new senior staff is impressed with our region. We had put together a 'killer' marketing promotion that we thought he would like, but when we presented it, he said the new team had better marketing plans for the future. I am hoping those plans will include me … at corporate."

"Are you going to ask him about it today?"

"I think so. We'll see how it goes. He is new to his job and I do not want to push him, but I will definitely ask him at some point. I think it is time for me to get off the road and into a position in the company with less traveling so I can spend more time at home with you."

Dana squeezed his leg.

"That is much better than a pinch." He smiled. "Where in the world does this guy live?" he said, changing the subject. "We are starting to get into the high-rent district now."

"I thought everything in Malibu was the high-rent district."

"I know…" he hesitated. "It is."

Both of them sat quietly for a few minutes absorbing the scenery. They were traveling north on Southern California's famous Coast Highway, just passing the prestigious home of Pepperdine University, which sat high on the bluff to their right. To their left was the world's most trendy coastline. The fabulous view was a magnet for Hollywood's elite: Mel Gibson, Barbara Streisand, Whoopi Goldberg, and Tom Hanks, to name a few. But Malibu had been attracting stars since the early 1930s when the silent film originals like Ronald Coleman, Clara Bow, and Gloria Swanson made their homes along the famous stretch of beach.

"Dana …" Daniel paused in amazement as he turned left onto a road leading to the famous Point Dume State Beach. "How could he ever afford to live here on **POP's** salary? This is incredible."

Daniel continued driving past the iconic homes, surrounded by upscale landscaping. Many were highlighted with coastal evergreen shrubs that were designed in spirals, shapes of animals, and even an angel. They continued down the hill in the direction of the ocean until they reached Westward Beach Road. To their right were homes and to their left was a sheer cliff overlooking the rocky shore. Most of the houses were newer and sat to the right of the road while only one was set on the left, on an outcropping, close to the edge of the cliff. It was older and out of place, but had a circular driveway in the front.

"This is it?" Daniel said, flabbergasted. "How in the world could he ever afford a place with a view like this?" He looked up the beautiful coastline toward Oxnard and Ventura, twisting a bit in his seat to see the shoreline down to Santa Monica. "Malibu has to be the highest priced real estate in the country … and on a cliff overlooking the ocean? I don't care how old and outdated the home is, it must be worth millions."

"He must be from money. Maybe he inherited it."

"I guess. There's Mack now." He pulled his car to the side of the driveway and waved. Daniel opened the car door and stepped out as Mack walked toward him with his hand outstretched.

"Daniel … welcome, I am glad to see you, and this must be Dana," he said, walking over to give her a hug. "I am glad to finally meet the woman who has captured this guy," he said, slapping Daniel on the shoulder. "He has told me about you," he lied. "Come on in. Carole is in the back setting up for the barbecue."

The three walked through the Art Deco cottage which hinted at a bygone era. It was evident that at one time it had been an attractive beach house, but its sparkle had clearly faded. The living room featured a gently sloped vaulted ceiling with exposed beams. At some point, the entire side facing the ocean had been replaced with oversized sliding glass doors that stretched from one wall to the other. It released from the middle to either side of the room, leaving the area of the home facing the water almost completely open to the veranda. As they walked outside, the view became spectacular.

"Hi, Daniel … Dana," Carole said, smiling. "Welcome. I am glad to meet you two, especially Daniel," she said, smiling. "My husband has many good things to say about you."

"Thank you. That is nice to hear." Daniel smiled to her, then to his new boss. "You have quite a beautiful home. Thank you for inviting us over."

"Beautiful?" said Mack. "The view is beautiful, but the house is about to fall over."

"No, it's not," Carole slapped her husband playfully on the arm. "He wants to tear it down and build a new one."

"Yes, she is right. The house is grandfathered in the city's zoning and one of the few homes built that remains this close to the cliff. The newer homes, like the ones across the street, have to comply with the new codes, but not this one."

"I don't know. I think it is quite nice just like this," Dana said, looking around.

"Oh my gosh!" Daniel had walked to the railing facing the ocean and looked down. "Dana, look at this. The whole deck extends out over the edge of the cliff."

Dana peaked over the edge, moving slowly backward toward the house, causing both Mack and Carole to grin and chuckle a bit.

"Don't worry about it, Dana," Carole said. "Right after we had it built,

I had to inch my way to the railing. I'm glad to see I am not the only one to think of the long drop to the water under the deck."

"The deck is new?" asked Daniel. "I thought you just moved in."

"We did," said Mack. "This was the first change we made."

"You will soon find that my husband does not let too much grass grow under his feet once he starts something," Carole added.

"I will make a mental note of that." Daniel smiled at Mack, who took up where his wife left off.

"I read a book about a baroness in Italy who, in the late eighteen hundreds, built a deck extending forty feet from the side of the hill her home was built on. She would breakfast there every morning watching the peasants working in the fields below, with the Ionian Sea as the backdrop. It was one of the first decks to be cantilevered over a precipice like that. This seemed like a perfect setting to do the same," he paused, "over this ..." He gestured with his hand at the incredible ocean view and the waves striking and breaking against the rocky shore below.

As if on cue, a seagull having caught an updraft soared at eye level only a few feet from the deck, observing his curious onlookers. Cawing loudly before leaving, it then rode a downdraft toward the rocky shore below as Mack and Daniel peered over the railing, thoroughly enjoying the spectacle. After a few moments, Daniel continued the conversation.

"You are talking about the Baroness of Bologna."

"Yes, I am. Sorry, I am used to telling it to people that are not familiar with franchising," Mack said. "of course you would know the story, Daniel."

"Yes, I do. I have read the book as well and think I could tell the story in my sleep. I recount it to new franchise owners at almost every grand opening." Daniel turned his attention to the girls. "Peppino was the son of the baroness and came to the United States in the early nineteen hundreds. With family money, he began helping his friends get started in their own restaurant business featuring Italian recipes and specializing in pizza. As they began to make money, he would take a cut from each restaurant, using a portion of the profits to advertise their name promoting all their locations and a percentage to expand his own locations."

"**Peppino's Pizza** wasn't the first pizzeria in New York," interjected Mack. "That title actually goes to Lombardi's which opened in 1905, but it was one of the first. As we know it." He added, "AND they still use the same recipe."

"Yes, you are right, Mack. You have done your homework," Daniel said, smiling, "Actually, the first franchises started in Germany in the 1840s, with beer companies giving licenses to taverns to sell their ales. Peppino's success was his housekeeper's recipe for great pizza, and the fact that he was an honest business owner helping his friends. Much like Will does with **POP's** franchise owners."

"I didn't know that, Daniel," Dana remarked. "Peppino's Pizza? It kind of has a ring to it."

"I didn't know any of this," Carole added. "I just knew that Mack read a book about a baroness with a deck which extended out from the house over a cliff and he had to have one. He was talking with architects as soon as we purchased our home and it was completed before we moved from Chicago."

"How did you have time to do that? I thought you were just hired a few …"

Mack interrupted. "Daniel, let's leave the girls to get acquainted and I will give you a tour of the property," Mack said, extending his hand to show him the way to the bluff beside their home.

"The property, you mean there's more?" Daniel said, surprised, forgetting to finish his last question.

"Yes, that is what made this home so attractive to us. It was built in the early 1930s and sold recently by the heirs of Clara Bow, a silent movie star. It had been in her family all this time. It came with about a hundred yards of cliff-front property." Mack gestured proudly toward the long and narrow piece of craggy ground. It was bordered by the small road on one side and the cliff's edge on the other. "The land is unusable for building; otherwise, some developer would have snapped it up for condos, but this is just what we wanted. I plan to build a small vegetable garden right here in the spring." He kicked his shoe into the loose dirt.

"I'm impressed. You must have done quite well for yourself before coming to **POP's**."

"Yes, I have. I was fortunate to get a good job with **BBI.** They have treated me well. They treat all of their employees quite well, as I am sure you will find out."

"That brings me to my question." Daniel hesitated before continuing, choosing his words carefully. "I know quite a few of your coordinators are married and still on the road constantly, but I am not sure that is what I want to do after I get married. Do you think there would be a place for me in corporate?"

Mack looked at him with a noncommittal look. "When are you two getting married?"

"Sometime next summer. We haven't set the date yet. Dana has been married before, so there won't be any big wedding, but afterward I would like to move back to LA. She has a teenager and a home here. I think it might be easier for them if I make the move so she doesn't have to."

"It's very considerate of you, Daniel." He paused, "A teenager, huh? Are you sure you know what you are getting into?"

"Tad's a good kid. We'll make it work. Besides, I think it would be fun to be back here at corporate full-time again."

"I understand you were Assistant Advertising Director when you started with the company."

"I was. Then it seemed we grew to the point there were a number of owners with special needs. Will thought it would be a good idea for me to go into the field for a while to help get the struggling marketing coordinator program back on track. So, there you have it. But it was never intended to be a permanent thing. Mack, I really like **POP's** and I hope to be with the company for the rest of my life."

"I really enjoy your sincerity. I now understand what the franchise owners see in you. You are the link that helps keep them together." Mack said in a teasing way, "I am getting the impression that if **POP's** didn't have you around, the company might fall apart."

"I wouldn't say that, but what I am saying is that I want to be a part of **POP's** future and that future is now with **BBI**. Let's just say I'm committed to the growth of **POP's Office Supply** and the success of its franchisees."

"I have heard all you have said, Daniel, and I will keep it in mind. I will pass this along to the senior staff and to **BBI**." Turning and changing the subject, Mack said, "Now let's get back to the barbecue before the ladies start to miss us. Besides, I would like to introduce you to the light of my life, my four-year-old daughter, Rachael."

"Okay, and thanks, Mack. Seriously, welcome to **POP's**. I am glad you are here."

The two men started back to the house when Mack's cell phone started ringing. "It's Tim. Hold on for a moment." They both stopped and Mack turned his back to the breeze as he answered. "Hi, Tim. What's up?"

Daniel could see Mack's body tense and his facial expression changed to concern.

"Where are you now?" he asked Tim and then listened, straining to hear him with the sound of the ocean in the background. "Okay, yes, Daniel is here with me. We'll both be there as soon as we can. We're leaving now." He hung up.

"What's going on? What happened?"

"The storm last night wrecked the office building. Tim is over there assessing the damage. He said it is extensive. We had better get there right away."

"Sure, I'll get Dana and say goodbye to Carole and we will follow you."

# CHAPTER 4

D aniel pulled his car into the parking lot following Mack's BMW. "It looks fine. I wonder what all the fuss is about. I can't see any damage at all," Dana said.

"Tim told Mack that the air conditioner went through the roof, but you are right. I don't even see a broken window." Daniel parked his car in the employee spot and applied the brake. "I'm going to check it out with Tim and Mack. Do you mind waiting in the car?"

"No, take your time. I'm fine."

Daniel made his way to the entrance where his bosses were talking. "Hi, Tim. What's going on? How much damage is there? It looks pretty good from out here."

"Yeah, well … looks are deceiving; there is quite a bit of damage on the inside. The air conditioner went right through the top floor and into my office. It's a mess." They entered through the emergency stairwell from the parking lot. "The electricity is out, so there is no elevator. I don't know how this could have happened. This is a brand-new building and is supposed to be able to withstand an earthquake. I'm going to sue the builder and he is going to be sorry he ever heard the name **POP's** by the time I am finished with him."

Both Daniel and Mack remained quiet as Tim angrily made his way up the stairwell to the fifth floor where the executive offices were located. He talked constantly, demeaning everyone from the builder, the city council, and the mayor, as well as the insurance adjusters who were certain to be a pain and damning them all for this inexcusable interruption to their business.

Daniel was starting to get out of breath as they reached the Executive Suite level and entered into the Administrative lobby. For a moment, everything looked just as it had when he left the day before. All the offices on this level lined the perimeter of the building, giving each of them a view of the Agoura Hills and allowing convenient access to one another. On one corner was the elaborate conference room, with floor-to-ceiling glass from the inside lobby lying shattered among bent pieces of twisted steel. Part of the ceiling had fallen on top of the forty-foot redwood conference table, collapsing its legs on the far end.

The wall that housed the electronics had completely collapsed in upon itself, crushing much of the digital equipment. TVs, mega computer screens, projectors, WI-FI modems, high-end cameras, and recording equipment lay mangled. This was the nerve center that allowed the executive staff to have meetings with employees in the field as well as franchise owners in their place of business, both in the USA and internationally.

Many times Daniel had used his smartphone to project his face into this room and onto the huge screen that was now cracked and bent out of shape. Sometimes if there was a major meeting, the team would get together where they would be able to see the senior staff, but most of the time it was only the senior staff that could see them. He always felt uncomfortable with that arrangement, but it was merely a downside to being in the field. He looked at wires strewn everywhere from the digital wall that now was only partially standing.

"Be careful where you step," Tim said as he cautiously walked across fragments of slippery broken glass toward what remained of his office. "How could this have happened?" He lamented again. "We have only been in this building three months. Everything is brand new and ruined! Look at my suite." The door was stuck ajar, but Tim took his foot and, in a momentary tantrum, kicked it open further so they could all see the damage.

Daniel was amazed at what he saw. It was only yesterday he had been in the lavish office, visiting with Tim and giving him an update on his region. Now it was in total ruin. The walls on three sides had collapsed completely. Broken glass and pieces of drywall were strewn everywhere, the cherry-wood floor rippled, cracked and split in places, but the most unusual sight was what Daniel could see directly in front of him, and he was speechless.

The enormous air conditioner had crashed through the roof, traveled through the employee gym and lounge on the top floor, haphazardly scattering treadmills, ellipticals, and exercise bikes everywhere, some still hanging precariously from the gigantic hole in the ceiling. But the most mesmerizing was the air conditioner itself. It had fallen through on an angle, with one corner smashing into the top of Tim's desk. It had landed so hard that the desk had collapsed in the middle, creating what looked like an enormous V from where he was standing. Although the rest of the room was demolished from the collapse, the desk was the only piece of furniture that it hit. Yet while everything else around it was crushed, the air conditioning unit itself appeared to be in a fairly good shape.

"Look at this place! It's going to take months to get this fixed." Both of the men could see that Tim's face had turned red with anger. "Mack, get hold of some real estate agents and find temporary office space immediately. Rent some furniture and get movers here." He paused. "Get these files out of here … and get the computer guys here quick. All the corporate data is on those machines," he said, pointing to one of the broken PCs.

"Calm down, Tim," Mack said. "All the data will be okay, it is backed up. The franchise information is safe. I will get a team to start assessing the damage right away and get the information to you as soon as possible."

"Good, make it happen and make it fast," he ordered.

"What can I do to help?" asked Daniel.

"Nothing here. You get back to your region and keep business as usual. We don't want the owners to feel they are inconvenienced in any way by this catastrophe. You are good at that. Get on the phone with your team and the owners and let them know we have it handled."

"Sure…" Daniel turned as he heard the sound of broken glass being crunched to see his friend Greg along with another man approaching.

"Hi Tim, Mack, Daniel," he said, nodding to each one soberly. "This doesn't look so good."

"That's an understatement!" Tim snapped. "Who is that you have with you?"

"I'm Curt Wisely." He reached out his hand. "I am the insurance claims adjuster." He handed Tim his card and showed him his credentials. "I've been going through the building trying to get some estimate figures for you."

"Good, thank you for coming so quickly." Tim shook his hand warmly and professionally. "How long do you think it will be before we can get all this fixed and be up and running again?"

"I can't give you a time on that, but from my experience with a building this big and with this much damage, I would say at least three to six months … but that is a very rough estimate. I have a lot of work to do before I can ascertain what needs to be done"

"So what caused all this? Was it the storm last night or something else?"

The adjuster smiled. "You mean like a bomb or something? No, nothing nefarious from what I can tell so far. Although I haven't completed my investigation yet, I am pretty confident from what I see that it was caused by the storm last night, in which case it will most likely be classified as an Act of God."

"What does that mean?" Mack asked.

"It is an insurance term which means you are completely covered for damages. You will be fine and glad to know that my company works very efficiently. I should have some solid figures for you in a few days."

"Good, get them to Mack here," Tim said. "Greg, I want you to work with Mack in finding us some temporary headquarters."

"Sure, I'll get right on it." Greg nodded.

"Greg," said Mack, "go down to my car and we can start getting some initial plans together. I will follow you in a minute. Daniel, it was good to see you and I think it best you be on your way back to your region. I will keep you informed. I want you and your guys to spend the next few days calling every one of the owners and let them know we have it all under control."

Daniel and Greg started walking back to the stairwell, crunching glass as they moved across the litter-strewn work area. As soon as the door closed behind them, Daniel turned to Greg. "Did you hear what the adjuster called it?"

"What do you mean? It wasn't a bomb, if that's what you are saying."

"No, not at all. He called it an Act of God."

"Yea … so what? That's what they call it when it is caused by natural events. It's the legal term," Greg said, "That's all."

"I know that …, but Greg …" Daniel looked at his friend, expecting him to get the implication.

Greg stared back. "What, I'm lost, what are you getting at?"

"You know… Act of God!"

"Daniel, sometimes you can sound so ridiculous. Don't go getting religious on me."

"It has nothing to do with religion. As you said, it was a natural event caused from the thunderstorm. I'm just wondering why God is so pissed."

"Daniel, you ARE ridiculous," Greg said, starting down the steps, complaining. "The company is thrown into turmoil and you are blaming God … or whatever. You sound nuts!"

"I am not nuts, what, you don't believe in God?"

"You're such a jerk. Only you could turn something like this into …" he hesitated, looking for the right words, "something like that."

"You know, if you were twice as smart you would be stupid, and don't call me a jerk …"

"I could eat a bowl of alphabet soup and poop out a smarter comeback than that."

"Daniel," Greg said flippantly, "you only annoy me when you are breathing."

The two continued to quibble and trade insults all the way down to

Daniel's car, where he stopped to say hi to Dana. She rolled down the window.

"So what's going on? How bad is it?" she asked.

"Pretty bad. There is no way they can do business here for a while," Daniel said. "The top two floors are trashed."

"Too bad, how did it happen? Was it from the storm last night?"

"Yea, the insurance adjuster thinks it is. He is calling it an Act of God."

"An Act of God. What's He so pissed about?" asked Dana.

"Oh, you too. You are too much!" Greg said, shaking his head and smiling while he backed away to leave. "You two are M-F-E-O!" He said each letter distinctly while turning and waving to them with his hand in the air. "See ya!"

"Greg, wait, what's M-F-E-O?" Dana asked loudly.

"Made For Each Other ... didn't you see *Sleepless in Seattle*? You two are Made For Each Other!"

"Thanks," yelled Dana.

Greg continued walking without turning and lifted both hands in the air and then let them slap back down to his side without turning. "WHATEVER!"

# CHAPTER 5

Franchise Conclave
Atlantic City Convention Center
Atlantic City, New Jersey

Some of the small business owners traveled by shuttles that looked like old-fashioned trollies, while the more energetic made the trek by foot, stopping for a **Starbucks coffee,** passing stores like **Tommy Hilfiger**, **adidas,** and **Banana Republic** while on their way to the opening presentation of their Franchises' Conclave. It was an exciting time and the electricity in Atlantic City added to that enthusiasm. From the moment they arrived, they had been made to feel special. As the thousands of cars, buses, and limos exited the expressway, they were greeted by **Caesars Hotel and Casino's** enormous and brightly lit million-light-bulb billboard. The animated display depicted an eagle flying out over the ocean and then returning with an American Flag hanging from its beak. With a flick of its patriotic head, the lights transitioned into an American flag as huge as the sign and then began to sparkle and dissipate, transforming itself into the words ATLANTIC CITY WELCOMES POP's Office Supply, the words morphing into a map of the Unites States with a thousand stars brightly pinpointing each location. Then steadily, one small light increased in size until it took over the entire board, lighting up the surrounding intersection like a nova. Immediately, it appeared to evaporate, becoming smaller as it reduced into one tiny light, which grew again, this time transforming into the Statue of Liberty, its lights sparkling and changing into the colors of fire, ultimately becoming the flame in the great lady's torch. Lastly, in one explosive crescendo of lights, it evolved into a world map with flags unfurling, indicating POP's many international locations.

Every franchise owner who experienced those moments felt an intense sense of being part of something bigger than themselves. And this was at the moment of their arrival and only a harbinger of things to come.

As the hordes of people entered into the convention center lobby, they shook off the late November chill and friends greeted one another with shrieks of recognition and laughter, many not having spoken since the last gathering. Those that took the time to look above their heads were given a sense that they had entered into an invisible aquarium. Hanging from the ninety-foot-high, sky-lit atrium were five colorful flying fish sculptures, incorporating all who stood below into an undersea world of the marine art.

Loudspeakers crackled over the noisy clamor and then a woman's voice welcomed the group and announced the start of the session in ten minutes. At that, the assemblage began funneling their way through the doors and into the auditorium.

Greg Martinez, Senior Sales Manager, made his way through the crowd to the first row where most of the speakers were gathering for their turn at the podium. Greg was a handsome man of Spanish descent, whose air of charm seemed to exude from a depth of sincerity, an unusual quality for a salesperson, but then not so different from what the franchise owners had come to expect from **POP's**.

He spotted Daniel Davidson, Marketing Manager, standing off to the side talking with one of the franchise owners. The two teased each  other incessantly having grown into a mutual respect for one another professionally, but because of the diversity of their positions, they locked horns now and then. Even though both had graduated the same year from San Jose State University, neither knew each other until **POP's** brought them together. Daniel was a bit younger, and with his unpretentious, tousled light-brown hair and sometimes youthful naiveté, except in business, seemed somewhat younger than his early thirties. Over time they had become like brothers, incorporating all of the familial qualities which included standing up for each other in public to bickering in private.

Greg envied Daniel's natural ability to navigate almost any situation with the franchise owners and admired the way they responded to him. If it came out of his mouth, they believed him. That's why he needed him to believe what he and a few of the owners had to say.

Moving next to him, he placed a hand on his shoulder. Daniel shook hands to say goodbye to the man he had been talking with and then turned his attention to Greg.

Greg spoke just loud enough to be heard over the hubbub. "Daniel, we need to talk. Can you get away?"

"Hey, Greg, what's up?"

Looking around to make sure he could not be overheard, he lowered his voice and said, "It concerns the new senior staff. There's something not right about them."

Daniel turned away from Greg and, unseen to him, pursed his lips and then turned back smiling. "I have to give a marketing seminar in about an hour or so, can it wait?"

"Not really. Look, I know you are behind the new senior staff, but you have to keep in mind that it was a hostile takeover."

"I fully realize that, Greg, but hostile takeover only means that **POP's** was purchased by a company that bought the controlling shares and decided to have their own men run the company." Daniel shrugged. "If I spent millions on a company, I would want to run it the way I wanted to as well. Give them a chance Greg, will you?"

"Look, a few franchise owners approached me with the same concern I have and they would like you to meet with them while Will is speaking. I have not told them my own thoughts about the senior staff and I think it is best we keep it that way."

"Are they the complainers?"

"On the contrary. Dottie, Sam, Lance, all friends of yours. They want you there and it would be wise to hear what they have to say."

"Dottie Daye will be there?" Daniel moved around a bit uncomfortably in his seat before answering, as she was a good friend and a well-respected franchise owner, as well as the vice president of the Franchise Owners Association. "Can't it wait? Will is the next speaker and I don't want to miss what he has to say about the transition. This is the day he is officially turning over the reins to the new guys. Greg, he has been one of the pioneers in franchising, respected by the whole industry because of his accomplishments and integrity." He gave him an irritated expression and continued, "Why would they pick this time to meet?"

"They chose it because everyone will be in the session to hear what Will has to say, and it is unlikely the ones that aren't there will be missed. They know it is a delicate situation and they assured me that they have not mentioned their concerns to any of the others."

"I'm not sure I like the sound of this." Daniel turned his attention to the podium as he heard Tim adjusting the microphone, then looked at Greg holding one hand up, indicating that he did not want him to speak for a moment.

"And now I want to welcome the man you have all been waiting for," said Tim Morrison, "the man who fathered more than 2,000 **POP's Office Supply** franchises in the United States and around the world. A man revered within the industry as one of the forerunners of franchising, the POP from **POP's** …, Mr. Will LaTrove!"

As Will and Winnie walked onto the stage, more than two thousand couples and their key employees stood on their feet to greet them. All had big smiles, loud applause, and a few friendly catcalls.

Daniel turned to Greg. "All right, I'll stay a few minutes and then try to slip out. There is a fifteen-minute break after Will and then I go on with my marketing presentation." He spoke loudly enough to be heard over the applause. "Where is it?"

"Here in the Sheraton, room 1051."

Daniel looked at Greg and shook his head. "What are you getting me into?"

Greg shrugged and gave Daniel a slight grimace, indicating he was not sure himself, then left while Daniel turned his attention to the podium.

Finally, the applause started to die down and Will waved his hands, indicating for them to quiet down as he began to speak.

"I want to thank all of you, but with a welcome like this, I am just not sure what to say."

Winnie, Will's wife, who was sitting on the speaker's platform, cupped her hand around her mouth and said loudly to the crowd, "Boy, have I heard that one before." At that, the convention floor went into uproarious laughter.

Will turned toward Winnie, smiling, and with a chuckle in his voice, he said, "Would you like to come up here and give the talk?"

"Why, do you need help already?" she quipped while smiling at the audience.

The crowd laughed again. Will turned back to the gathering, repressing his laughter. "What can I do? You all love her and I can't live without her."

Someone yelled good-naturedly from the crowd. "HENPECKED!"

At that, Winnie stood up and walked across the stage and took the microphone from her husband's hand. "Who just called me a hen?"

Again the crowd went into a fit of laughter. Will took the microphone back and wrapped his arm around his wife and addressed her. "Can I get on with my talk now, please?"

Winnie smiled at her husband and her friends in the crowd, which were most of them, and pretended to be reluctant as she returned to her seat.

"Now you know what I have to put up with every day," he said, laughing. "But in all reality, our relationship has gone through what many of you have experienced. A number of you left good jobs and were thrown into a totally new profession, not to mention being flung into a situation where you were working with your spouse for the first time. That is tough on any relationship. Just like many of you, Winnie and I had difficult times learning to work together, but it finally evolved into what it is now, a comfortable situation. She became your Public Relations Director because she told me that working with me was the only way we were going to get quality time to spend with each other. Little did I know how good she would be at the job." He waited while the applause sounded throughout the room.

"But that is not what you came to hear about. Winnie and I are retiring and you have a new team of executives looking out for you. This Conclave is not about us, but a look to the future with your new leaders, and I would like to bring them up to the podium, one by one, to give you a chance to know a little about each of them. Let's start with Tim Morrison, your new President ..."

Daniel stood, halfway bent over as his cell phone vibrated. He reached into the inside pocket of his Ralph Lauren suit and held it close to his ear. "Yes, who is it? I'm in a loud place, so please speak up."

"Daniel, this is Lance Schiffold. I just wanted to make sure you are coming."

"Yes, I'm on my way now. I'll see you in a few minutes."

"Good, we're all here waiting."

Concern crossed his face as he made his way out of the audience's line of vision to the stage, then he stood straight. Winnie caught his eye and he smiled back and gave her a silly distorted facial expression, at which she smiled and rubbed one of her index fingers over the top of the other, as in "shame on you." Daniel smiled back to his good friend and made his way out of the auditorium.

Unknown to him, Joe Farrow, Executive VP of POP's, had come off the stage and walked over to where Mack Costello, the VP of Marketing, was sitting. He took the empty seat next to him, then leaned over whispering, "Where's Daniel going, Mack?"

"I don't know. I thought he was here."

"No, he took off. Something must be going on for him to leave during Will's talk. Keep an eye on him. Make sure he doesn't get together with

Dottie Daye. From what I heard, she could be a problem. She has a lot of sway with these people and so does Daniel."

"I'll talk to his team and find out."

"Do you know if it is true that Dottie had a heart attack last year?"

"Yes, I did hear that, why?"

# Chapter 6

Daniel got off of the elevator on the tenth floor and walked down the corridor to room 1051. He noticed video equipment monitoring the hallway and was glad that POP's always held their meetings at top-notch locations. Atlantic City was chosen because it had one of the largest expo centers in the eastern United States as well as the beach and boardwalk for the family and casinos for parents. Even though the city had taken its lumps in recent years with the spread of legal gambling around the country and the close of many of its own gaming hotels, the excitement somehow remained in the air. He felt fortunate to be part of such a good company as he knocked lightly on the door.

Greg welcomed him with a smile. In addition, he was greeted by three franchise owners: Dottie Daye from Texas, Jerry Jones from New York, and Lance Schiffold from Michigan.

"Hey guys, what's up?" Daniel asked while admiring the beautiful suite. To his right, three steps led to an elevated bedroom surrounded by railing. It overlooked the comfortable living area which included two sofas and a wingback chair in front of smoked mirror tiles that gave the room depth. Daniel walked straight to the oversized picture window and stood for a moment looking out over the island toward the famous boardwalk and the ocean, before turning toward them with a warm smile.

"Nothing to be alarmed about," said Dottie. "There are probably some reasonable explanations for the questions we have and we're hoping you can give us some clarification."

"Fine, but why me?" he said, turning and taking a seat in the wing-back chair, realizing that it was left vacant for him and understanding the implication.

"Because we know you will give us an honest answer," Lance offered, and the other three nodded in agreement.

"Well then, tell me what's going on," he said, leaning forward just a bit with a seriously concerned look on his face.

Dottie looked at the others for a moment and then started. "We have concerns about the new senior staff. But first, let me try to summarize the positives."

"Thank you. I really would appreciate that," Daniel said a bit uncomfortably, and added, "I like positives." He smiled at her.

"Sales at my locations are up fifteen percent since last year," she said.

"Mine is up about ten percent," Jerry offered, "but I'm not complaining."

"No complaints about sales. At least at this point," added Lance.

"Sales for new franchise locations are up as well and all of you know stocks for the company are heading in the right direction," Greg added.

"BUT ..."continued Dottie, pausing, "we have been hearing some rumors that the new senior staff has been making special deals on franchise territories with some of the new owners in Texas."

"Whoa, wait a minute." Daniel sat up, tensing a bit. "That is a serious accusation and one I doubt is true." Daniel said, concerned, "Territories are a very sensitive issue with all owners and the new executives were hired because of their extensive business backgrounds. I am sure they are very mindful of that." He paused, realizing that this conversation could turn volatile if not handled wisely. "Listen, you guys," Daniel said, shaking his head in disagreement, "they would be shooting themselves in the foot. A franchise is sort of like a big family and information like that has a way of getting out and spreading quickly. If it were true, it could bring down the company and I seriously doubt they would be so stupid. These guys are all pros and we should be happy to have them taking over for Will.

Come on, they have only been running things for a few months. Let's give them a little time."

"Regardless, can you find out if it is true?" Dottie asked.

"Look, I am the Regional Marketing Manager for about one-third of the USA and that includes Texas. If it happened in my territory, I would have heard about it already, and I have not heard a thing."

"You are hearing about it now," Lance said.

"Yes, but it is all conjecture. I doubt Will would approve a new president that would do something like that. **POP's** is his baby and I am positive he would have checked each of them out thoroughly. I'll make a few calls, but I am sure you are wrong."

"Daniel, you do know that Tim was not Will's first choice, don't you?" Greg said softly, and then looked at his friend.

"No, I didn't," said Daniel.

"The way I heard it was that the one he had chosen was offered another job a few weeks before coming on board with **POP's**, so Will was forced to hire his second choice. That would be Tim."

"Hey, come on, you guys are really reaching," Daniel said, defending Will's choice of a new president. "I will check out your concerns and let you know, but for the time being, let's just keep this between us. I'm serious."

"Okay," offered Lance, "but if there is truth to it, we are not going to take this sitting down."

"I hear you loud and clear. Now we better get back to the conference to hear the last of Will's talk. It was good to see all of you again," Daniel said, slapping his hand on his knees and bringing the meeting to a close.

The owners shook hands with Daniel, and Dottie gave him a hug. As the others walked to the door, Greg tapped Lance on the shoulder and asked him if he and Daniel might use his room for a moment. He nodded and Greg then indicated to Daniel that he should wait.

When the door closed, Greg was the first to speak.

"Daniel, I think the rumor they heard is just the tip of the iceberg," he said, leafing through his briefcase and pulling out a booklet. "I did not share this with them because I thought it might add fuel to the fire. Here is the new company prospectus that lists the senior staff and their respective backgrounds. I got a copy of it after it was printed and before the decision was made not to send it out to the franchise owners before Conclave."

"Why would they print it and not send it out?"

"Take a look at this." He opened the brochure to the page listing the new executives and pointed to the background of the new president. "Tim's background shows he worked for a franchise that declared chapter eleven, bankruptcy."

"No way!" Daniel said, grabbing the prospectus out of his hand to take a closer look. "I don't know much about the stock market, but I know that when a company files for reorganization, their investors take a hit. "Will would never go for that."

"Maybe that's why he was not his first choice. Now look at the vice presidents that he brought with him. Most of them have worked for companies that went chapter eleven as well."

Daniel looked at Greg, hesitating while trying to decide if he should tell him or not. "There is something I did not mention to you at lunch last week. While I was at headquarters a few months ago, I just happened to stop by Will's old office when I heard him yelling. I'm not positive who was with him, but there were several people. I don't know what it was about, but Will was angry."

"Was Tim in the meeting?"

"Yes, I did hear his voice. But I have never heard Will so angry. I am serious," he said, thinking back. "I remember one time he was so annoyed that he threw papers across his desk at me and another time when we were in the lobby, he got so pissed he took some papers out of my hand and threw them on the floor before storming out the door. Unfortunately, I have pushed his buttons on a number of occasions, but I never heard him like this … never this angry."

"You serious? Did you really do those things?"

"That's nothing," Daniel said with a slightly embarrassed smile. "I have gotten him fuming at me many times. Even on my job interview," he said, giving in to a chuckle as he thought back.

"Get out, you got him angry during your job interview? Only you could do that," Greg said in disbelief while shaking his head, "and get away with it!" Unable to stifle the next question which had nothing to do with the current situation, he asked, "Then what did you do?"

He shook his head slightly before answering, finding it hard to believe that he had really done it and wondering again what Will had seen in him that day and why he was hired for his previous position as Assistant Advertising Director. "Well," Daniel scrunched his face a bit as he thought back before answering. "You know sometimes when you meet with him he makes you sit in a very long and uncomfortable silence without saying a word?"

"Yea, he does that a lot."

"It's part of his strategy. He gets you to divulge something you had not intended to say … and it works. There he is sitting at his oversized desk with nothing on the top of it but his pad and paper, jotting notes about my interview. After about a minute of a very uncomfortable silence, he puts the pen down and reaches into his drawer for something. That's when he's got you. You know you must say something to keep his attention and then out it comes, everything you didn't intend to say, but the things you were hoping he didn't find out when checking your references. He still gets me with that tactic, and I even know it's coming." Daniel smiled. "Now I use it in my own interviews."

"You are a piece of work, Daniel," Greg said, enlightened and now understanding what was going on during his own conversations with Will. "So, what did you tell him?"

"Seriously, Will had me so nervous that I started listing my weak points, one right after another. I'll never know why I did that, but it was the only thing I could think to break the silence. Among the litany of faults, I told him that sometimes I put off getting things done until the last minute, but then proudly told him that I always get my work done on time. It was like I heard myself saying the words in disbelief and still couldn't stop."

"I bet he loved that!"

"Are you serious? He got angry. He raised his voice and in a firm tone asked me why I would come to an interview and try to convince him that I was the man for the position by trying to sell myself using my bad points. Then you'll never believe what I did."

"You're probably right, what?"

"I figured at this point I had lost the job. He raised his voice at me so I thought it fair to raise my voice to him."

"Get out of town, you got angry with him … during the interview … and he still hired you?" Greg was shocked.

"Yes, I told him that I had already given him my strong points. If he was a good interviewer, he should be trying to uncover my weak points because those would be among the qualities he would be hiring. I walked out of his office and into an interview with Winnie, who was the Public Relations Director. She asked me a question that I thought stupid, so I told her what I thought, and then I am pretty sure I gave her one of my 'are you seriously stupid' looks."

"You told Winnie off?"

"Well, not exactly told her off, but she knew where I stood. When I left, the Advertising Director, who was my initial contact, said to me, 'Don't call us, we will call you.' Are they famous last words or what?"

"That's amazing!"

"Yes, it is. They had over two hundred applicants for Assistant Advertising Director. Before I left, I was sure I didn't have a chance. I had really blown it. When I got home, an hour later they called me and offered me the position … and that, my friend, is a true story!"

"Unbelievable!"

"Yes, then after I was hired, I would go to lunch with Winnie and to dinner at their home occasionally. They became like a second set of parents. You know something, never once in all the times I made him angry was I ever afraid he was going to fire me." Daniel looked at Greg with a concerned look. "All this to say that I know Will, and I know his anger, but that day at corporate he had a different kind of anger. One I had never seen before. I thought it must have been his having a hard time letting go of the reins of the company ... but now ..." he paused, not knowing how to finish the sentence.

Greg looked at his watch. "I don't know what to make of it either. We'll talk more, but we best get back to the seminar."

Daniel looked at his watch. "Yes, I better get going."

It was evident Will had finished his talk, seeing franchise owners talking in small groups as he made his way down to the auditorium. He took longer than usual as he was stopped by a number of owners that wanted to say "hi" and had a quick comment or question to ask. When he arrived, it was almost time for his presentation. He was arranging his props next to the podium when his new boss approached.

"Are you ready?" Mack Costello, the new Director of Marketing, asked.

"Sure, I enjoy making presentations."

"Good. I was looking for you a while ago. Where did you go?"

Daniel answered without skipping a beat. "I needed to go to my room and pick up the props for my session. I waited until Will started introducing the new senior staff before I left."

"Did you talk with any of the owners?"

"Yes, I ran into about ten of them on the way from my room, Mack. Why the third degree? I am a little busy at the moment."

"No problem. Good luck with your lecture."

"Thanks, but I'm not counting on luck. Like Will has taught all of us. Be prepared!" Daniel tapped the microphone to make sure it was working and it caused a screech that caught everyone's attention. He nodded at his boss with a smile, before Mack retreated to his seat in the front row.

"Good afternoon," he said, uncharacteristically serious. "I know you are in this session to learn marketing techniques, but I want to say something about Will LaTrove." He turned away from the crowd for a second, covering his mouth with his hand to conceal an uncontrollable smile and then turned back to the audience with a serious look and continued.

"Will, you are well loved by all these franchise owners, but there is something they do not know about you … and it is something I want to personally say before you retire." Daniel looked down at the floor then shook his head side to side. "I can't think of any other way to say it then to come right out with it. Will LaTrove … you're a sucker!"

More than two thousand people went completely silent while Daniel looked at the crowd and kept telling himself, wait … a little longer … almost … "And so is Winnie … and Ann and Rick over there …" He pointed to two of the well-known owners. "And even Dottie Daye over there. Even she is a sucker." She was sitting on the aisle a few rows back and gave him a questioning look. The silence continued as everyone tried to figure out what was going on. He paused.

"Most of you know the guys from my region, they are sitting right here in the first row. Hi, John. Hi, Stephan, Susan," he said, addressing each of them and exchanging smiles. "You may be experts in market-ing, but you guys are suckers, too! Me, I am a sucker, too! Do you want to know why?" He could tell by the relieved looks he saw on their faces that he had everyone's attention, just as planned. He waited for a moment before continuing.

"Because, every time you shop for groceries or go to Walmart, you are manipulated by marketing strategies." Everyone in the audience let out a breath of relief, glad that it was all part of Daniel's performance. "That's right," he persisted. "Didn't you ever wonder why the staples that you purchase frequently are located in the back of the store? There is a reason. Have you ever noticed that when you go in for milk and bread you come out with other things you hadn't planned to purchase? It's true, right?" The audience murmured their agreement. "You go in to buy five dollars' worth of groceries and come out with a forty dollar bill. Sound accurate? The end caps offer you products at a special price that's just too good to pass up. All the aisles you walk by on the way to the bread and milk remind you of something else you needed, or just a plain great deal. So, you see that makes all of us suckers … not just Will and Winnie. That's what this marketing session is all about. We are going to learn how to market to our customers, what impulse buying is and what trips your customer's trigger to make an additional pur—"

Daniel paused mid-sentence as he noticed Dottie Daye, who was sitting in the second row, standing and looking at him with a peculiar expression. She then gurgled loudly and fell sideways, over her manager's legs and into the aisle. "Dottie, are you all right?" he said into the mike as he rushed off the stage and to her side along with several other people who were already kneeling next to her. "Someone call 911! PLEASE!" Daniel yelled. He lifted her wrist into his hand to feel for a pulse, and finding none, he placed two fingers on her neck. With a distraught look, he turned to Will and Winnie, who had rushed to their side. "I can't find a pulse. I think she might be dead!"

# Chapter 7

Evening After the Conclave Ended
Atlantic City, New Jersey

A soft knock on the hotel-room door interrupted his thoughts as he lay on the bed resting. Most of the franchise owners left the day before and he assumed it must be one of his marketing team, most likely John, who was also a close friend. But he was not in the mood to talk with anyone and was dressed only in his gym shorts. He had not even wanted to talk with Dana when she called earlier. He was in total confusion, trying to examine the barrage of conflicting thoughts that were assaulting his mind.

Irritated and uttering a sharp expletive under his breath, he shot off the bed, trying to control his temper before he reached the door. He exhaled quickly, trying to regain calmness, then took another breath and pulled it open.

"Melinda," he said surprised and immediately self-conscious and wishing he had his shirt on. "How are you?" He stood with the door ajar, but not opening it all the way. "I would invite you in, but as you can see, I am not dressed."

"That's okay," she said, pushing the door open a bit further while grabbing the waistband of his gym shorts and giving him a stimulating look. "Neither am I."

Instinctively, Daniel backed up, which he immediately realized might not have been such a good idea as she was now in the room with the door clicking shut. She began to brush her hand on his bare chest.

Completely caught off guard, he grabbed her hand and pushed it away. "What are you doing?"

Melinda had been holding her knee-length jacket closed with one hand and now allowed it to part, revealing her silky, thigh-high, pink negligee.

"Melinda," he said angrily, "stop this!"

Convinced that all men were desirous of her and confident of the sexual prowess she could exercise over them, she took her fingers and again started brushing his chest lightly with both hands.

Daniel could feel his desires starting to give way, but did not reveal it in his voice. "Melinda, I am sorry if I did anything to make you think I am interested in you. I like you as a friend and that is all."

"So then you ARE gay?" she said, continuing to stroke his torso. "I wasn't sure."

Figuring that might be the best way out of the situation, he responded: "You may think what you want, Melinda, but the truth is that I am just not interested in a relationship with you."

"Who said anything about a relationship?" she said, taken aback. "I just thought it would be a nice release after the intensity of this past week."

"Well, that is not necessary and I think you need to leave now," he said, taking her firmly by the shoulder while opening the door. "Let's just pretend this did not happen." He was firmly pushing her into the hallway and closing the door.

Regardless, his sexual trigger had been tripped and momentarily was unable to control the sense of arousal he was feeling. *I have got to call Dana,* he thought. He reached for his cell phone, and moments later she answered. "Dana, you are not going to believe what just happened."

"What's wrong?"

"A beautiful woman knocked on my door and wanted to have sex with me!" He said it in a teasing way with a smile in his voice.

"Daniel, get over yourself, you're not THAT good-looking."

"Why, you don't think another woman would find me attractive?"

"Sure, I do. Never mind. What's going on?"

Somehow the desire to tell her what had happened immediately disappeared. "Nothing important, I am just getting ready for bed. I leave in the morning and called to say good night."

"All right, good night, talk to you tomorrow."

"Yeah," he said, disconnecting her. *What a crazy week this has been*, he thought to himself, flopping onto the bed and pulling a pillow up tightly to his chest and hugging it until he finally went into a restless sleep.

The following morning, Daniel packed and then rested for a few minutes in the wingback chair looking out the window. POP's employees were all given twelfth-floor rooms, each with striking views of the ocean and coastline. Daniel leaned back into the leather armchair and lifted his legs onto the ottoman without breaking his stare. He was raised in Ventnor, a small city on the beach a few miles away. He leaned forward, looking down-beach toward the Ventnor Pier a few miles away. He was thinking how much his life changed after moving to the west coast right before his senior year of high school. This was the first time he had returned home in several years. Yet because of the Conclave, there was only time for a quick dinner with his parents and brother and his wife. They all understood and he frequently spent time with them at his lakefront home in Florida anyway, as it was often their vacation destination. Now, he was not unlike the millions who visited the famous resort each year. After college in Northern California, he had moved to Los Angeles where POP's corporate headquarters became his home, and the owners and the people he worked with, his family. He hated moving to Florida as regional manager, but it was necessary at the time. Now he impatiently waited for the chance to come back to Los Angeles.

His thoughts disappeared with a grimace, jolting him back to the present, thinking of his friend, Dottie Daye. The paramedics had come to find only a slight pulse. He was informed that she was in critical condition at the **Atlantic City Medical Center** and had fallen into a coma. The prognosis was not good.

The new team, however, insisted that the conclave continued. He was able to muddle through his presentations, but it was difficult. He could hear the words coming out of his mouth and yet his thoughts were of Dottie. Thinking back, she appeared restrained when he saw her with the other owners. It was like she was trying to will him into understanding what she was saying … yet it was only implied by her body language; her voice remained calm, steady, and controlled. Now, her warnings about the senior staff kept nagging him. Could she be right? Were they somehow corrupt? But for what reason? Were the owners and Greg onto something that he was refusing to see? Yes, he questioned their abilities in marketing, but never their intentions. But if it bothered Dottie so much that she had a heart attack over it, she must have really been convinced. He must try to understand it as she understood it. He breathed a silent prayer asking for clarity.

When Will first mentioned that he was going to make POP's a publicly traded company, it made sense. They would have an inflow of cash to help expand the company and it certainly gave the franchise an elite status. With Will at the reins, there was no doubt the company would grow with integrity, but it was becoming increasingly clear that this new regime was implementing a different kind of business than he had been used to. Now it seemed the focus was on fast growth and profit and the bottom line and less on helping the owners. Daniel trusted Tim simply because he was Will's choice as president, but then he found that he had not been his first choice but his second one. The first had accepted the position and then changed his mind a few weeks before he was to start work. *Who would do that?* he thought. *Could there be something devious there? Could it be my silly imagination?* Daniel scrunched up his face tightly while bringing his hands to his face and vigorously rubbing his eyes in frustration. He suddenly stood up, blurting out an unintelligible sound and walked to the suitcase lying open on the bed. He was starting to pack more clothes in it when his cell phone started chirping.

"Hello," he said calmly while gathering his composure and answering in his business voice.

"Hey, Daniel, Lance Schiffold here."

"Hi, Lance. How are you doing?"

"All right, but I am still pretty shaken about Dottie."

"Yeah, me too. I had a hard time getting through the rest of the sessions."

"I know, I could tell." He paused. "Daniel, I do not think it was an accident. I don't have any proof, but my gut is telling me there is something more to it."

There was a lingering silence as Daniel considered his words before deciding to answer frankly. "I know, I have the same feeling, but I cannot think of any reason anyone would want to hurt Dottie."

"Neither can I, but you are in a better place to try to figure it out than I am." He paused again. "Daniel, I'd like to pass along something my father taught me that has helped me countless times in business."

"What's that?"

"He told me that it is harder for an honest man to see the dishonesty in others, than it is for a dishonest man to see it. In other words, a dishonest man is looking for trouble, while the honest man is expecting honesty in return. Daniel, my gut is telling me that if you are going to figure this out, you need to consider everything from their perspective and not your own."

"Your dad sounds like a smart man."

"Yes, he was, Daniel. I really sense something dark about these guys."

"Well, I never tried to second-guess Will's decisions before because I trust him."

"Exactly, you didn't need to."

"Maybe ... and I say maybe you have a point. I hate that I am even considering this, but okay, I'll think about it. But I still doubt that there is anything deceptive going on."

"Just look at everything from their viewpoint and you may be able to figure it out." Lance paused and then added, "We have confidence in you, Daniel."

"Well, we'll see. I will be on vacation next week and I will give it some thought while I am relaxing and sipping margaritas by the pool and working on my suntan," Daniel kidded. Then his voice became more serious as he added, "But Lance, I hope you are wrong."

"I hope so, too, but I have learned that where there is smoke, there is fire. Give me a call when you get back to work. I would like to have you visit my locations. I am thinking of opening a fourth one in Kalamazoo and I'd like to show you the area and get your thoughts. Perhaps we can arrange a visit?"

"Okay, no problem ... and Lance, we need to keep this conversation to ourselves."

"I know that, and Daniel ... enjoy those Florida babes, but not too much. I hear you are engaged."

"Hmmm, yes, I am and you are right." Then he added slyly, "So, I guess I will just have to try to enjoy them only a little bit." They both laughed. "Have a good trip home and I will talk to you in a few weeks." Daniel broke the connection after he heard a goodbye, then stared at his smartphone for a few moments before placing it back in his pocket.

He was glad the Conclave was behind him and looked forward to vacation. He had considered spending it with family, but there was too much to think about and he wanted to be alone. He had assumed he would work at POP's for the rest of his life, but now he wasn't so sure. His mind was having doubts, but his heart was certain. Now it was only a matter of time until his heart convinced his mind what he needed to do.

Daniel clicked his suitcase shut, then let it drop to the floor and extended the handle. He made a visual sweep of the room, checking the bathroom for anything he might have forgotten to pack and then opened the door. He turned to take one last look at the ocean through the expansive window and walked out, hearing it click shut as he began to walk down the hall.

# CHAPTER 8

Daniel disliked the Florida humidity, but enjoyed his screened lanai, positioned a few feet away from the edge of a small, man-made lake which had become home to quacking ducks, swans, frogs, and the occasional alligator. He was lounging comfortably with his feet propped up on an ottoman, answering emails on his MacBook Air. He swatted a mosquito and looked at the familiar blood smear on his skin. No-see-ums, as they were aptly named, were biting midgets less than three millimeters long, rendering screens almost useless. As with everything during the past few days of his vacation, his thoughts were convoluted.

A unique ring and pop-up alerted him that his uncle was calling using his new iMac computer. He clicked the Accept button and smiled as his uncle's face appeared. "Hello, Uncle Sprandy ..., glad to see you are trying out your new toy. This the first time you called me on FaceTime since I showed you how to use it. Now we can see each other when we talk."

"Daniel, if I want to talk to you I can call you on the phone, and if I want to see you face to face I can drive two miles. I don't like all of this newfangled technology."

Daniel laughed good-naturedly. "Okay. Well, I am so glad you called no matter how you contacted me. Hey, how are you two doing?"

"Just fine, just fine. Aunt Beulah asked me to invite you over for lunch. She fixed your favorite, roast beef."

"Okay, sure, that sounds great. It will be nice to visit with you. What time do you want me?"

"Hop in the car and come on over now."

"Okay, I'll be there in fifteen minutes. Do you need me to bring anything?"

"Just yourself. We'll see you soon."

Daniel watched him trying to figure out how to end the call, letting out an expletive before his face disappeared from the screen. When he was told to relocate to Florida, his boss said he could move anywhere he wanted, as long as it was close to an airport. He immediately knew it would be West Palm Beach so that he would be near his favorite uncle. It had become a wise decision. Both he and his wife had been very good to him, and when the family visited, they always included him in the activities. Each were astute business people in their own right, so he was able to talk to them about work when he felt overwhelmed, like he did right now.

Sprandy had retired from being the manager of the prodigious **Renault Winery** in New Jersey and was credited with creating their "Pink Lady" cocktail, which became popular during the fifties and sixties. After his first wife's passing, he married Beulah, who owned a posh jewelry store on Worth Avenue in Palm Beach and was noted worldwide for her unique ability to string pearls so closely together that the knot disappeared. Together they had fun running the store while catering to the creative whims of the rich and famous. Daniel looked forward to getting their take on the problem at **POP's** and lunch would be the perfect time to share it with them. He hopped in the car and, seven minutes later, pulled into their driveway.

His uncle was in the greenhouse tending to his lavish assortment of orchids when he arrived, and immediately started walking toward him with a concerned look on his face. "Daniel, I had a rather unusual call this morning from a friend of yours. He asked me to contact you and have you call him back from my home phone. I asked him where he got my number and he said he knew we had the same last name and … googled me up," he turned his last words into more of a question, "whatever that means." Then he continued, figuring Daniel understood from his nod: "Do you know anyone by the name of Greg Martinez?" He watched his nephew's facial expression change as a deep furrow formed in his brow.

"Yes, I do, he is a friend from work."

"He said he did not want to call you at home or on your cell phone, but needed to get in touch with you right away. Here is the number he gave me." He reached into his pocket and pulled out a small piece of folded paper and handed it to him. "It sounded quite urgent," he added. "Is everything okay?"

"Actually, I am not sure. In fact, I planned to talk with you and Aunt Beulah about it anyway. I'll get in touch with him after lunch."

"About lunch, that was just a way to get you here, but Aunt Beulah is in the kitchen making you a sandwich. Why don't you use my study and we can talk after your conversation with him. We are both curious to know what is happening."

"Thanks, Uncle Sprandy." Daniel smiled, and changing the subject, he said while gazing around the greenhouse. "Your orchids are looking terrific."

"It's a lot of work. But I enjoy it," he said, pointing to a flowering vine that had attached itself to a tree protruding through the screening of the nursery's roof. "This one opened this morning." He pointed to a beautiful and uniquely shaped white flower. "It has such a delicate presence," he said, admiring it, "and smell the aroma." He waved the flower under Daniel's nose and waited for a response.

"Smells nice." He smiled, enjoying the moment. "It has a scent of vanilla."

"It should. Did you know that this orchid's seed pod is where vanilla beans come from?"

"Really?" He hesitated, genuinely surprised. "No, I didn't."

"Its blossom is only open for a few hours and its smell is uniquely intended to attract specific pollinators. In fact, many varieties have a relationship with a single type of stingless bee or hummingbird that visits the flowers for their nectar."

"You are an encyclopedia of information on orchids," Daniel said, laughing and realizing that his uncle might not have understood it as a compliment but a sign that he was talking too much.

"Yeah, well … enough of this. You better go in and make your call," he said, placing his hands around Daniel's shoulders and walking toward the house.

Daniel shut the door to the study which was decorated with furniture from a bygone era. He perused the musty library for a minute or so before taking a place in an old-fashioned executive swivel chair that was so rickety that he had to balance himself to keep from tipping over. As he called Greg on the outdated dial phone, he realized that this must have been the furniture from his uncle's office at the Renault Winery many decades ago.

"Hello."

Daniel could immediately tell from the uneasy tone of his friend's voice that something was wrong. "Hey, Greg, I hear you wanted to talk with me."

"Yes, I do. Daniel, I'm sorry about having to call your uncle, but we've got problems!"

Daniel leaned his elbow on the desk and started massaging his forehead. "Greg, I take it this has something to do with our conversation at Conclave."

"Yes, it does! They are going to kill the two of us. I am sure of it. You have to leave now. Do it, or you are going to be dead."

"Whoa, whoa, slow down, my friend," Daniel said, running his hand through his hair and trying to quickly think of how to respond. "Calm down, Greg. I can see this has certainly gotten to you." Daniel paused, hearing only the sound of his friend's frazzled breath on the other end. "Look, Greg, I am on vacation right now. Why don't you hop a plane and join me? Come on. It will be fun and we can talk this whole thing out. How about it, we can ride down to the Florida Keys and do some sailing. What do you say?"

"Daniel, Sam Salerno is dead!"

"Oh my God." Daniel was momentarily stunned. "How sad ... how did he die?"

"And so is Jerry Jones from New York!"

"What!" Daniel stood up, looking at the door while running his hand feverishly through his hair. "What do you mean they're dead?"

Greg's voice increased in intensity and panic as he continued. "They are both dead ... DEAD!"

This time it was Daniel that was speechless as fear took root in his stomach. "They were all at the meeting in Atlantic City," he said, mumbling under his breath and continuing with trepidation. "How did they die?"

"Jerry got in a car accident on the way to work this morning and Sam was in the Delta Airlines crash near Chicago yesterday. He never even made it home from Conclave."

"That is very sad, but it doesn't mean there was anything criminal involved."

"DANIEL ... and Dottie Daye? Yes, it all sounds like a coincidence, but I do not think it is."

"Okay ... okay, Greg, let's get a conference call going with Lance Schiffold up in Kalamazoo. He was at our meeting and I'd like to hear what he has to say."

"I already spoke to him last evening. He called me at home from a burner phone."

"What ... why?"

"When he and Andrea arrived back from the Conclave, they picked up their dog and kids from her sister's house then went home. Their garage isn't attached and as soon as they got out of the car, their dog started barking at them running around in circles like he was wanting to get their attention. Then one of the kids spotted a footprint in the mud next to the driveway. At first, Lance dismissed it until he got close to the backdoor and smelled a light scent of gas. He went inside and opened all of the windows and checked the water heater and found its pilot light had blown out, which at first he was thankful, until Andrea checked the pilot light on the gas stove and found it was off, too. Had Andrea started dinner without noticing it and lit a match, she would have blown all of them to smithereens. Daniel, not just him, but his wife and kids and their dog!"

"You're not serious!" he said, panic beginning to overtake him.

"The next morning, he heard about the plane crash and wondered if Sam and his wife had been on it. After he found that they were, he called Jerry. That's when he discovered that he and his wife were both killed in a car crash."

"Oh God ... Oh my God, help us, oh my God!" Daniel was drumming his fingers frantically on the table.

"Daniel, I have no idea what we are dealing with, but we've gotta both disappear for a while until we figure it all out."

"Disappear?" he was saying the word as if he was mulling it over. "What is Lance going to do?"

"He is going to take his family and do exactly that until we figure out what is going on."

"Where is he going?"

"I have no idea, he didn't tell me. He has an untraceable burner phone and that's what he called me on. He told me to get one, but that was AFTER calling me on my home phone. That's why I can't go back to my house. I dropped my car in the long-term lot at the airport and then took a cab to a friend's and borrowed his motorcycle."

Daniel squelched his fear trying to regain his wits. He knew that mistakes were made when based on emotion, rather than intellect, and that could get him killed. For the first time in his life, he knew that he was about to be tested in a way that, until then, was unfathomable to him. As he forced himself to focus away from the fear, it began to lessen for the moment. "Okay, look, give me your cell number and I will get one myself and then call or text you and give you mine."

"Okay, but I don't want you to contact me unless it is absolutely essential." Greg's voice quavered. "Who knows who is behind all this or why ... Daniel, if they can bring down a plane, they can sure track a burner phone somehow!"

"Bring down a plane, really, that is what you think?" Daniel was silent for a moment. "Well, if you are right, I know who is behind it and you were correct all along!" Daniel could feel the fear turning to anger. "After leaving the meeting, Mark cornered me and insisted on knowing why I wasn't there for Will's presentation. I blew him off by telling him that I went back to my room to retrieve something I needed. He pressed me for more, but I told him I was too busy preparing for my presentation to talk and asked him if we could speak about it later."

"Absolutely! You are right. I bet they got access to the hotel security system and scanned the floors to see where you were."

"Yes, good thinking, Greg, and they were able to get a list of everyone at the meeting and would have suspected Dottie's agenda for getting us all together."

"But how in the world could they get a plane brought down? And how big a thing would it be to have enough people to do all the other things? This is a company with a lot of reach, but what kind of company could be that big to do all this?"

"I don't know. We gotta take some time to think about all of it. None of it makes sense and maybe it is all a string of coincidences."

"Coincidences!" Daniel repeated. "Time to think!" he said. "Time to think ..." he repeated, unnerved.

"Daniel, you don't have time to think. YOU GOTTA GO NOW, MAN!" he said in an exasperated voice. "Run now, think later!"

"Actually, I may be safer here, at least for the moment. I told Mark I was going to Barbados for my vacation, so he does not know I am at home."

"Barbados?"

"I had reservations, but with all that happened at Conclave, I chose to stay home and rest instead. The irony is that thinking about the problem may have saved my life.... I can't believe I just said those words." Daniel shuddered that the thought could be real.

"He may know now, if your home phone is bugged and your uncle used it to call you."

"Thankfully, he called me from his iMac. He bought it a few weeks ago and I showed him how to use FaceTime. But you are right." Daniel felt a twinge of panic in his stomach and was trying to suppress it. "One tiny mistake like making a phone call could get us killed."

"Correct, now you are thinking! Have you used your cell phone?"

"No, in fact, it's turned off. I didn't want to take calls from the franchise owners while I was on vacation."

"Fantastic! Keep it off and assume they can track you on either phone. I looked up spying devices on the internet before I called you. Daniel, it is not hard to track someone nowadays. All they have to do is put an app on their phone, call your phone from theirs and they can track and even listen to every single call you make or receive. Have you gotten any hang-ups or wrong numbers recently?"

"Oh shoot, yes, I did, right before I left the hotel. My display read 'private' and did not show the number. They hung up as soon as I answered, so I figured it must have been a misdial."

"Daniel, buy a burner phone right away and then download an anti-spy app. It will tell you if anyone is tracking you. Don't answer any calls unless you know who it comes from."

"Greg, how can they track a burner phone? From what I see on TV, they can't track them. That's why all the crooks use them."

"I don't know, but they may be able to somehow. But if they took down a plane, I wouldn't put anything past them. Look, I'm exhausted. I gotta go. I need to think of someplace I can be safe. Daniel, I am scared."

"Greg, I want you to do what I tell you to stay safe. I'm going to be doing the same thing."

"Come on, this is not the time for a sermon."

"I am not going to give you one. It is just a lesson to keep my best friend alive. Greg, accepting fear is a choice. You must refuse to think negative thoughts if you are going to get through this. Kick them out of your brain. They will expect us to make a mistake and will assume we are afraid. Let's let them assume that, but let's stand strong against the fear. Fear makes people react rather than act and that will get us killed."

"Somewhere in there is a sermon. I know it, you turkey turd!"

Daniel could hear his friend snicker on the other end of the phone and smiled. "Glad to hear your insult, fart breath," Daniel teased back. "The truth is that, it is just common sense. People in fear make mistakes and we cannot afford to make a mistake with these guys."

"All right, good advice."

"And I will be praying for you," Daniel added, laughing.

"You, turkey wad. I knew it. I'm going to beat the crap out of you next time I see you."

Both of them were laughing when Daniel's voice became a little more steady and serious. "I'd like to see you try, Greg. I mean it, I would like to see you try ... be careful, my friend."

"You too, Daniel. Oh, and one last thing. If for some reason you are calling and there is something wrong ... I don't know ... some kind of danger and you can't talk, say the word Starbucks and I'll do the same."

"Got it, Batman," said Daniel.

"Okay, Robin."

"Hey, wait a minute, how did you get to be Batman and me Robin?"

"Your words ... you finally recognized the superiority of marketing over sales," he teased.

"Paybacks, Daniel, paybacks ... and when you least expect it," Greg said, drawing out the words.

Daniel took his number and hung up the phone, then committed it to memory by repeating it seven times. After gathering himself together for a few moments, he got up and walked back to the living room.

"Oh Daniel, it is so good to see you," Aunt Beulah said, clapping her hands together. "Have a seat at the table. I fixed you a roast beef sandwich."

Daniel smiled genuinely, as she said it with the charm of a 1950s Southern belle. He would have considered it dramatic, but was accustomed to the way she entertained with the epitome of Southern hospitality coupled with her own exuberant flair that he knew would carry over into the blessing over the meal. He gave her a kiss on the cheek before sitting down at the dining table.

"Only you could decorate a table like this for a sandwich," he said as he removed one of the napkins from its engraved silver holder. "Uncle Sprandy, does she serve you dinner like this every night? Look at this: table cloth, candles, crystal goblets, and napkin holders."

"Not quite, but close," he said, kissing her on the cheek before taking a seat at the head of the table. "Beulah, quit your fussing and come and sit down so we can hear what's going on."

"Why yes, Daniel, we are so interested to learn," she said, taking her seat across from him. Instinctively, she placed both her elbows on the table in a gracious way and then entwined her fingers under her chin, smiling sweetly.

Daniel could not contain his laugh and turned it into a compliment. "Aunt Beulah, you are one of a kind and I am so glad you are family." He then became more serious and told them about the odd way the new senior staff had been acting when he visited corporate headquarters in California, then the concerns franchise owners shared with him at Conclave followed by Greg's frantic phone call informing him of the deaths.

"How do you know they can tie you into all of this? Are you sure that you are a target?" asked Uncle Sprandy.

"Yes, I am sure. It would be simple for them to get a copy of the security tapes from the hotel and see who was at the meeting."

"Then you do need to disappear for a while." He thought for a moment. "I have an idea."

"I'm listening."

"Why don't you take a flight to Italy and see Toni? He is your cousin and being a lawyer, he will know what to do and can advise you."

"Uncle Sprandy, he only speaks Italian."

"I know that, I know that," he repeated, "but his wife Elisabetta was born and raised in England and can interpret for you. She did it for us when we were there a few years ago."

"And she is such a lovely person," interjected Aunt Beulah.

"That's right, I wasn't thinking. She interpreted for me as well when I was there." He paused. "It really does sound like a good idea, and it will give me time to consider all of this mess. I still cannot understand a motive for any of it." Daniel sounded bewildered.

"You will find out, Daniel. You are my brother's son and I have confidence in you."

"Uncle Sprandy, I hate to ask, but I am concerned that if I use my credit cards that they will be in a position to track my movements. Would you mind lending me a few thousand dollars until I get this straightened out? I will pay you back as soon as I get through this."

"Of course, and I do not think it would be a good idea to return home today."

"And your car," said Aunt Beulah, "we can take it over to my sister's and put it in her garage."

"Good idea, Beulah," Sprandy said, nodding. "Get on the phone and find what time the flights leave for Rome while we will head to the bank."

"Okay, thanks."

Daniel wasn't taking any chances as he did not want to make a reservation ahead of time in case someone was watching his movements. *How ridiculous,* he thought to himself, *but it is better to be safe than sorry.* He considered a nonstop flight from the Miami Airport, which was only about an hour or so away, but then that would be a little too obvious if he was being tracked. Daniel smiled inwardly considering how smart and cautious he was being. He looked for a flight without a waiting list so he could just show up at the airport and purchase the tickets before boarding the plane. He decided his best chance was a flight leaving West Palm Beach later that afternoon and arriving in New York in time to catch a Delta flight leaving JFK at 9:40 pm and arriving in Rome at 4:25 the following afternoon. After picking up the money from the bank, his uncle took him to a Walmart where he purchased a backpack and some shirts, trousers, and a few other necessities to keep him going for a few days. He then dropped him off at the airport, visibly concerned for his brother's son and wishing him luck.

Daniel had not told his uncle there was one more thing he had to do before leaving. His oldest team member and friend, John, was in West

Palm Beach visiting some of the South Florida owners that week, giving them a change of pace while he was on vacation. John knew nothing about what was going on and he wanted to keep it that way for his own safety and that of his team. The less they knew, the better off they would be, but maybe he could plant some seeds so that he would stay safe.

After calling the local POP's Office Supply and speaking to him, they agreed to meet for lunch at the Denny's restaurant near the shopping center he was visiting.

"Hey, Daniel, how you doing?" John said, reaching out to shake his hand. "I thought you were on vacation? Weren't you going to Barbados?"

"I was, but I've just been relaxing at home next to my lake for a few days recuperating from the hectic time we had at Conclave. I just thought I would join you for lunch to say hi since you're in my neck of the woods. Let's grab a table and then order some lunch."

"Sounds good to me. You paying?"

"Of course I am, smart-aleck," he said, smiling and gesturing him toward a table. After ordering, Daniel told John he had something to say and was telling him as a friend rather than a boss. "As you know, John, I have been with the company for many years and this transition is turning out to be harder than I thought it would be. Don't get me wrong, I'm not saying anything bad about the new team, it's just that it is a difficult transition for me with Will and Winnie leaving. So, I've been thinking about making some changes myself and I wanted to give you a heads-up so that when you hear it you'll know that I'm not leaving the franchise with any bad feelings. I hope you know how much I care about the franchise owners and all of you on my team as well."

"Of course, I do … we all do. I have to say that I am sad to hear it, but not surprised, and I wish you the best when you leave. Have you thought about what you're going to do or is it still too early to think about?"

"I'm not sure at the moment. I am thinking of starting my own consulting business, but I'll just have to see. I think I'll first take a year off and maybe I'll even try to write a novel which is on my bucket list. Either way,

I'm just going to take some time to relax. I hope you will keep my confidence and not say anything until the time I make the announcement."

"Mum's the word," he said, smiling.

"John, I'm telling you early because I'm hoping that you will be the one that will replace me in my position. Actually, I won't make that decision, but I will most definitely recommend you. The franchises will need someone who is honest and has integrity to help complete this change to the new team. I know we've all had some disagreements with them, but I am hoping that you will follow their orders without question and yet take a stand when it comes to the good of the franchise owner. So, I guess what I'm saying is that it's nothing new for you."

"I appreciate your vote of confidence. I still have some problems with the new team, but I guess over time they will start to blend in and life will become normal again."

"That's a good attitude, John. I hope you keep those thoughts."

They finished their lunch and said their goodbyes, and Daniel was off to catch his plane, not having a clue as to the trial of faith that was awaiting him.

Daniel sat in the waiting area trying to comprehend all the things that happened in the past few weeks ... and over the past few months, for that matter, considering how his relationship with Dana had escalated. Sprandy and Beulah had driven him to the airport and wished him the best. Beulah had taken both his hands in hers and shaken them affectionately. Uncle Sprandy placed his arm around him and said only two words. Words he knew would have to be his mantra for the foreseeable future. "Be strong."

He couldn't stop thinking that perhaps he might be wrong about everything. That his mind was playing tricks on him by connecting circumstances that had no association whatsoever.

When he purchased his ticket, he used cash instead of his credit card but was required to use his license as identification.

# CHAPTER 9

## 666
## Fallen Angels

Location:  Just North of Hades; Great Distance from Paradise
Lucifer:   Better known as Satan; Former archangel fallen far from Grace
Havoc:     Lucifer's Inferior

Originally handsome above most created beings, once known as a day star and the son of dawn,[1] Lucifer sat on his throne, adorned with every precious stone: the sardius, topaz, diamond, beryl, onyx, jasper, sapphire, emerald, carbuncle, and gold.[2] In his hand was a golden scepter.

---

[1] **Isaiah 14:12** How art thou fallen from heaven, O Lucifer, son of the morning! How art thou cut down to the ground, which didst weaken the nations!

[2] **Ezekiel 28:13** Thou hast been in Eden the garden of God; every precious stone was thy covering, the sardius, topaz, and the diamond, the beryl, the onyx, and the jasper, the sapphire, the emerald, and the carbuncle, and gold: the workmanship of thy tabrets and of thy pipes was prepared in thee in the day that thou wast created.

When he pointed it, his attendant Havoc knew exactly what was expected of him and immediately started gathering his regiment of soldiers. His attention was drawn to the miserable little man onboard the ridiculously slow form of travel. *A gnat that shall be squashed,* he thought to himself. *I shall have a few surprises waiting for him.* He followed that thought with an evil laugh until he turned to see his boss. When Lucifer smiled directly at him, he shuddered fearfully.

# 777
# God's Angels

Location:   Moments from Heaven
Melchior    Archangel (pronounced Mell-shy-or)
Haszik      Guardian Angel: Humility, faith, and obedience were his great
            character elements

The two angels, hearing the discourse, raised themselves high above the earth until they could see the entire coastline of the eastern United States and Daniel's jet traveling north over Georgia heading for JFK International Airport in New York City.

Instinctively knowing what to do, they quickly slid down an accessible air current until each was floating beside the windows of the plane.

Melchior was an Archangel who The Father trained in Holiness as a warrior along with Michael and Gabriel, among others. He was gifted with insurmountably pure wisdom and could bestow that gift liberally upon humans when requested.[3] He attended the birth of Jesus along with the Magi in Jerusalem more than two thousand years ago and was, as with all angels, messengers guided by their adored and precious Holy Spirit. Melchior was on the same level as the Seraphs and Cherubs who attended Father God in His tabernacle. Although these angels are equal in power, there was a difference in their administration. Archangels are the leaders of the hierarchy, so they have an army of angels who answer to them. However, Seraphs and Cherubs are not involved in administration and they do not have angels under them—they stay in the presence of God, eternally worshiping Him and are considered blessed above all other angels.

Haszik had been on assignment with Daniel since the day he was born and prayerfully entreated Melchior for the privilege of assisting him through his Dark Night of the soul. Haszik was a witness to many of the sinful acts Daniel had done in his lifetime, but had grown to love him anyway because of his prayerful and repentant nature. He had been charged with testing his integrity many times and once even appeared to him in the flesh as a stranger needing help.[4] Unbeknown to him at Daniel's birth, his own angelic nature would be especially helpful on this assignment. Haszik is a bold name, spiritually describing confident courage that is perfected during trial. Its origin conveys the recipient to be strong and take hold of courage and not give up during the chaos and storms of life.

Haszik smiled at Melchior. "I know why I am here now," he said, looking at Daniel, who was sleeping with his head resting against the airplane's window. He smiled back knowingly and nodded as they both moved into position. Melchior knelt down on his knees, straddling the wall separating the cabin from the wing of the plane, and Haszik positioned himself in the empty seat next to the one he loved and guarded with all his strength.

---

[3] **James 1:5** If any of you lack wisdom, let him ask of God, that giveth to all men liberally, and upbraideth not; and it shall be given him.

[4] **Hebrews 13:2** Be not forgetful to entertain strangers: for thereby some have entertained angels unawares.

Anointing oil appeared on his finger as he moved his hand toward Daniel's forehead and then he spoke in a heavenly language being interpreted as, "Take this courage, my friend," saying this as he invisibly touched him. "I give you access to these qualities as you go through the horrific storm you are about to enter." He then said each word distinctly and strongly: *strength, stamina, endurance, perseverance,* and *fortitude.* "You will only obtain them by faith and anything less than faith is sin and separation from God which will allow access by the enemy of your soul.[5] I pray that your faith may increase and be perfected in the Mighty power of God. Rest now and take heed to the words and images that you will see, being careful to test each one, making sure they are of the Lord.[6] And when you do, follow each instruction carefully, never leaning to your own understanding.[7] You will not see us, but we will be close by. But you must remember at all times not to hamper our help by your doubt." The two messengers then quoted the Word of God in unison … both as a prayer and a warning. *But let him ask in faith, nothing wavering. For he that wavereth is like a wave of the sea driven with the wind and tossed. For let not that man think that he shall receive anything of the Lord. A double-minded man is unstable in all his ways.*[8]

Then, in the twinkling of an eye, their already invisible forms disappeared.

---

[5] **Romans 14:23** And he that doubteth is damned if he eat, because he eateth not of faith: for whatsoever is not of faith is sin.

[6] **1 John 4:1–2** Beloved, believe not every spirit, but try the spirits whether they are of God: because many false prophets are gone out into the world. Hereby know ye the Spirit of God: Every spirit that confesseth that Jesus Christ is come in the flesh is of God.

[7] **Proverbs 3:5** Trust in the Lord with all thine heart; and lean not unto thine own understanding.

[8] **James 1:6–8** But let him ask in faith, nothing wavering. For he that wavereth is like a wave of the sea driven with the wind and tossed. For let not that man think that he shall receive any thing of the Lord. A double-minded man is unstable in all his ways.

# CHAPTER 10

Daniel awoke to the familiar sound of the jet engines' whine and aware of a dream that gave him a sense of foreboding. He smiled to the man sitting in the aisle seat of his row and then closed his eyes again, leaning his head back against the window. He watched the wisps of clouds flitting beneath him. But this time it was not sleep he needed … it was courage. *Lord, it just occurred to me that I have not been praying a lot over the last several days. I am sorry. Please help me remember all of the dream I just had and as I repeat it to you, I prayerfully ask that you will somehow find a way to confirm to me that it was from you. If it really was then I ask for the interpretation.*[9]

*I saw myself in a small village running down a winding cobblestone street. On either side were villagers standing in their homes, each behind a Dutch door with the bottom half closed, so that I could only see the upper part of their bodies. I felt fear and the cobblestones were making me constantly trip, so I had to catch myself in order to stay on my feet to keep running. Their faces were expressionless, like they were wondering what I was doing. I reached a small park with three huge willow trees. Each with long, drooping branches that looked like tears that almost reached the ground. They started swaying as the wind picked up and I ran across the grass toward the one in the middle. The wind suddenly became wild just as I reached the blowing*

---

[9] **Genesis 41:1** And there was there with us a young man, a Hebrew, servant to the captain of the guard; and we told him, and he interpreted to us our dreams; to each man according to his dream he did interpret.

*branches that were now whipping back and forth. I caught one and it flung me toward the tree trunk. I wrapped my arms around it and was hanging on for dear life when the wind became stronger and my arms weaker. I finally let go and found myself picked up and swirling through the air going further and further from the ground. I could see others with frightened looks on their faces and animals and a roof blowing past, missing me by inches. Then as fast as it started, it stopped and I dropped out of the wind, but now I was high above the ground … the church steeple in the middle of town looking so small. I began to fall faster and faster, writhing in terror until suddenly I landed in a farmer's field into the middle of a haystack. I sat there catching my breath and looked at the swirling clouds not more than twenty yards away circling around me and realized I was now in the eye of a tornado.* This is where I want to stay, *I thought. I picked up a piece of hay and stuck it in my mouth and then I woke up.*

The pilot came on announcing their descent into JFK International Airport, followed by the airline attendants walking the aisle to make sure everyone was securely fastened in their seat belts. Daniel felt rested as he walked off the plane and into the busy concourse. He stopped in the men's room which was jammed with other passengers deplaning their flights and smacked into several people who were hurrying on their way out while he was making his way in. Forgetting that his backpack stuck out about a foot behind him, he turned quickly to excuse himself for bumping into someone and ended up slamming it squarely into another man who literally pushed it out of his way almost causing him to lose balance. The rude man didn't even turn toward him as he hurried past.

From there he headed directly to the Delta International ticket counter. So far he felt pretty safe and hadn't noticed anything unusual. He waited until the last possible minute before queuing. By the time he reached the customer service agent, he had about an hour to make it through security and to the boarding gate. He thought about taking his backpack onboard with him and stowing it in the overhead bin, but decided against it at the last minute and watched it move away on the baggage carrier behind the counter, wondering if he made the right decision.

*Too late now,* he thought, as it disappeared with the other luggage heading for the plane.

By the time he reached the gate, the plane was almost finished boarding and Daniel found himself at the end of a group of about twenty-five men and women dressed impeccably in high-end business attire.

"Are you all with the government?" Daniel smiled as he asked the man around his own age standing next to him.

"The government? No," he replied, smiling, "but we all work for the same company."

"You look like you are dressed pretty much alike. The last time I saw something like this I was in North Carolina just after the President's jet left and the plane I was on was packed with Secret Service agents returning to Washington. It was hard to tell one from the other. I remember thinking that they didn't look so secret to me."

They both laughed.

"It's funny you say that because I thought the same thing when I arrived this afternoon ... even to the red, white, and blue tie," he said, lifting it up a bit. "Actually, it's a little embarrassing. We all work for the parent company of Carrier. They make air conditioners and heating and cooling systems. We are on our way to an international sales meeting and that's the reason for the red, white, and blue. One of the PR people thought it would be a good idea for everyone coming from different companies to wear their country's flag colors so we could tell each other apart."

"You're kidding?"

"I wish I was," he said with a smirk. "Besides Russia, France, and England, do you know how many other countries that have red, white, and blue on their flags?"

Daniel laughed. "No."

"Neither do I, but at least they all have different patterns." He returned the laugh. "You know those marketing guys, they gotta come up with some gimmick to make their bosses happy."

"I know what you mean. I work with marketing guys, too!" Daniel added, "Where is your conference? Rome?"

"No, I think the company was afraid if they held it in Rome, no one would show up for the sessions. It's going to be about two hundred miles north in Pisa. They will have a van waiting when we arrive at the airport to take us the rest of the way."

"Oh, you're going to like it there," Daniel said. "I visited Pisa a few years ago. There is a lot more there than the leaning tower. Plus the Italians are interesting people and very friendly and helpful."

"Ah … it'll make no difference anyway. We have a full schedule, but I am sure it will be fun and I am looking forward to it. The parent company we work for, Comfort International Associated, always takes good care of us."

"You're kidding me … CIA? You do work for the government!" he said, teasing him.

"You got me. We get that all the time." He laughed. "By the way, what's your name?"

"Daniel," he said, stretching out his hand.

"Mine is Jim." He accepted Daniel's hand and shook it.

They both boarded and wished each other a good trip. The plane was packed and Daniel made his way back to his window seat in row twenty-one. He was glad to see that the other two seats were vacant. After taking his shoes off and putting on the complimentary slippers he found in the seat-back pocket in front of him, he grabbed the onboard magazine and started paging through it. A few minutes before the appointed time of departure, the pilot came on the intercom apologizing and informing them that there would be a thirty-minute gate delay.

After the thirty minutes had passed, the flight attendant announced that they had been informed the delay was due to the late arrival of a connecting flight and that those passengers were expected soon and asked everyone to please be patient.

About ten minutes later, five men boarded and walked down the narrow aisle, occasionally bumping their carry-ons along the way. No one said a word as they passed, but every eye was on them. The first was a heavy-set, older Italian-looking man dressed in fine casual clothes that were too tight for him as his belly drooped so far over his belt buckle that it was completely obscured. Daniel couldn't help but notice that he had an angry look on his face and found himself staring at the man as he passed. Evidently, he had caught his eye as he returned it with a cold look. The two men behind him were younger and appeared muscular and fit, while the two behind them were a couple of good-looking men about his own age. They stopped at his row and the first one looked at the two seats next to Daniel and said, "Sorry, guy, it looks like you're gonna have some company."

"Not a problem," he said, removing the magazine he had laid on the empty seat.

"I'm Stefan and this is my friend Lance," he said, taking the middle seat.

"Nice to meet you," Daniel said cordially, noticing that both of the men were impeccably dressed and wearing expensive tight-fitting clothes that he wished he could look as good in.

"Are you going to Italy on vacation or business?" asked Lance as he unbuttoned his shirt and then leaned forward to stow his small carry-on under the seat in front of him, giving Daniel a view of his now exposed chest inside his taut shirt. "Do you guys think it is hot in here? I'm boiling."

"I'm fine," said Daniel. "It'll probably get cooler when they start the engines, and in answer to your question, a little of both." He was watching as Stefan leaned against the seat and lifted his body while brushing the wrinkles off of the top of his slacks. Noticing that neither of them was wearing a wedding ring, Daniel got the impression they were gay. "How about you two?"

"We're off on a vacation," Lance offered, brushing his hand through his shoulder-length dark hair.

"We're looking for some fun for the next few days," Stefan said with a warm smile. "How about you?"

"I'm going to be visiting some family and checking out a few places to take my fiancée on our honeymoon," Daniel said.

"Really, when are you getting married?" Stefan asked with interest.

"Ahh … next summer is the plan. I want to surprise her with a trip to Italy, and I'm going to check it out first to make sure everything will be perfect. She has no idea I am gone for the next few days." Daniel turned to look out the window for a few minutes trying to understand what was going on and remembering the words that Melinda said to him when she showed up at his room. "So you ARE gay," she had said. At the time, he remained silent and did not respond. *Could this have anything to do with that?* he wondered.

Suddenly, a sense of foreboding overtook him. *No, I'm connecting dots that aren't real,* he thought to himself forcefully, refusing to give in to the unfounded fear that was beginning to overtake him. He turned back to the two men, who were both looking at him, and returned their smiles before resting his head on the window. Outwardly, at the moment, he knew he looked calm, but before turning his head away from them, he had glanced at their hands again and noticed that Stefan was now wearing a wedding ring.

Daniel kept his head against the window with his eyes closed. His mind kept bringing up thoughts that seemed to link one to another. Some were associated with work and some unrelated, like the man who bumped into him in the men's room a few hours before. At that moment, a strong thought came to him almost like a warning. *Act, don't react!* It was like a command coming from his subconscious that was aware of something he wasn't.

*I hope Haszik is working today,* he thought, inwardly smiling.

About a decade before, he had taken a few years off from **POP's** to work with an ad agency in Philadelphia as an account executive on their **McDonald's** restaurant account. He wanted to learn what he could from the top American franchise, in the hope that Will would then rehire him and he could return with more expertise, which was exactly what happened. He smiled remembering that on the day he returned to work, the elevator door opened and there was a sign in front of the doors that read, "Welcome Back, Daniel." He laughed and immediately knew that must have been the work of his good friend Winnie LaTrove. Boy was she good at public relations, he remembered. And boy did that feel good.

His work with McDonald's was interesting, and by the time he left, he had learned the lessons he wanted. It had been better than his years at college because he knew exactly what would help him in the franchise industry. But there was one memorable yet unrelated incident that occurred during that time.

He was responsible for all the locations in central Pennsylvania and had rented a home in the outskirts of Hershey. The town was so small it had only one traffic light, but it was an absolutely beautiful place to live and leave from each morning, traveling the Pennsylvania Dutch Country while visiting with the various McDonald's owners. He and Dana were long-distance dating at the time, talking on the phone almost daily. His evenings were free, so he took classes from an organization learning how to become a foster parent and furnished his second bedroom with two double beds for teenagers that needed a place to stay on occasion.

One February, he was returning from a week's vacation with his family in Ventnor. It was almost midnight when he approached an isolated intersection in the road. As he took the left turn, his headlights shined on a young man hitchhiking. He was not in the habit of stopping to pick up strangers by the side of the road, especially at midnight, but he had seen few cars for the past half hour and this man wasn't even wearing a jacket and the temperature was about seventeen degrees and dropping.

He clicked the button to unlock the passenger door and will never forget what happened next. The man leaned his head in with a smile on his face and said hello. That was expected, but what was unusual was the look on his face. Daniel paused a second, not being able to recognize the expression, before returning the greeting and telling him to hop in.

As he pulled back onto the road, he asked the man where he was going and was told that he would like a ride as far west as possible. That was when Daniel realized he had a problem. The next twenty miles was a highway that ran in the middle of farmland and he would be turning off of this road onto another at a desolate intersection in order to get home.

There weren't even any gas stations along the way where he could drop him. At that moment, he realized he was about to do one of the most stupid things he had ever done.

"What is your name?" Daniel asked.

"My friends call me Haszik."

"Haszik, that's an unusual name."

"Yes, I know, but it's actually quite common from where I'm from in an area east of Europe."

"Okay, anyway, I just realized that between here and my home there is no safe place to drop you off and I live in a really small town where there aren't any services or even small stores along the way."

"Oh, I see," he said, not sounding at all concerned.

"But I have an idea. I don't want to leave you stranded in this freezing cold without a coat, so how about I take you home with me? In the morning, I can call my pastor and maybe he can help in some way or I can drop you off in Hershey where you surely will be able to find a ride."

"That would be very nice of you," he said.

*Very nice and VERY stupid,* he thought, rebuking himself. *DANIEL, WHAT ARE YOU DOING!* In the darkness of the car, he was unable to examine him more closely to see if there was any indication that he might be dangerous. When they finally reached his home and had walked into his living room, he noticed the same look on his face that bothered him when he first opened the car door. But perhaps he was wrong. He really just seemed a little confused, or even mentally challenged, but either way, definitely in need of help. He would talk with his pastor in the morning.

Haszik took a seat on the floor next to the coffee table. "Are you hungry?" Daniel asked. "Would you like something to eat?" Then he remembered that he hadn't gone shopping before he left for vacation and the only thing he could offer him would be a peanut butter and jelly sandwich.

"Sure," he said. "You know what I would really like? Do you have a peanut butter and jelly sandwich?"

Daniel stood staring at him for a moment before disappearing into the kitchen, praying. Daniel returned with the sandwich and then realized he had to tackle the next predicament ... where was he going to sleep?

If he went upstairs to his own bedroom and let him sleep on the sofa, he would be able to clean out the house and be long gone before morning. Rather than leaving him in the living room, he decided to let him sleep in the room he often housed foster kids. Their room had two beds in it that were already made up where he could sleep.

Finally, Haszik was in his bed, and Daniel was in the bedroom right next door. He left both doors open so he would be able to hear him if he got up, but still he was worried that he could be murdered in the middle of the night after he fell asleep, so he was doing his best to stay awake. The waves of sleep were just starting to flow over him when suddenly Haszik appeared at his doorway, nearly scaring the bee-gee-bees out of him, and announced he was going to be leaving.

"Oh, okay, that is fine with me if you really want to," Daniel said, tossing off his covers. "Let's get you on your way then." He then got out of bed fully dressed and put on his shoes and went back downstairs.

As he headed to the front door, Daniel said, "Hold up a minute," and went to the hall closet, returning with a jacket. "Here, put this on, it will keep you warm."

Haszik put it on and turned to look at Daniel with one hand on the door knob as he was about to leave. "Daniel," Haszik said, "you have done everything that is expected of you even to giving me your cloak."

Daniel stood there shocked at his words and watched as he disappeared, closing the door behind him. The moment he clicked it shut, he was able to identify the expression on Haszik's face. It had been the look of a parent adoring their new baby. It was a look of adoration. At that moment, he knew that for the rest of his life he would never forget the night he entertained an angel unaware.[10] He honestly did not know if he was a real angel or not, but he did know that inwardly, when he thought of his guardian angel, his name would be Haszik. *Besides,* he thought, *it*

---

[10] **Hebrews 13:2** Be not forgetful to entertain strangers: for thereby some have entertained angels unawares.

*had been a dead giveaway when he referred to the jacket as a cloak. Who would do that?*

Now it was time to figure out what was going on with the two guys next to him. He sat up turning to them with a smile.

Stefan looked at Lance and then back toward Daniel. "You woke up at the right time. The hostess is bringing dinner around."

"Great, I'm starting to get hungry, thanks." Daniel thought of a Bible verse that he committed to memory because it had been difficult for him to understand, let alone implement. Matthew 5:44–46: *But I say unto you, love your enemies, bless them that curse you, do good to them that hate you, and pray for them which despitefully use you, and persecute you.* Unbeknown to the two men, Daniel prayed for them, not knowing what evil was to befall him within the next few hours.

"Hello, gentlemen." The flight attendant grinned nicely. "Are you three traveling together?"

"No, these two are … and I am solo," answered Daniel. A while later, she returned with their meals. "Where are you all headed?" she asked.

"Rome," answered Stefan. "My friend and I are here for some fun. Would you like to join us?"

"Oh, wow, what an offer," the hostess said, smiling like she had fielded the same question a hundred times before, "but I'm afraid my husband wouldn't like that at all. But thanks for the offer."

"You sound like that guy," Lance said, gesturing toward Daniel. "He's here on a pre-honeymoon trip looking for places to take his wife after the wedding."

"Now that sounds romantic," she said, truly interested. "Where are you going to be looking?"

"I am thinking about Pisa. I have been there before and the area surrounding it is beautiful."

"You're absolutely right," she said emphatically. "The entire Lombardy region is amazing. Everywhere you look is like a picture post card. I'm sure she will love it. Good choice."

"That's what I remember. The Italians take their food and wine seriously. I was never stuck for somewhere to enjoy a good meal and Lombardy is full of small family-run hotels and restaurants. I just want to make sure I find the perfect ones."

"Oh," she added, topping off their coffees, "and I'm sure she'll love all the quaint little villages with cobblestone streets …"

Cobblestone streets?

"Yes, they are all over the place. I wish you the best and hope you enjoy your honeymoon." Then she moved on to the passengers across the aisle.

After dinner, Daniel paged through a few magazines and then took out his Kindle trying to find a book to occupy his mind, but it wasn't working. He glanced at his watch … *a little more than four hours from New York … halfway there.* He started playing around with a scenario he could implement if there was a problem, which at the moment he did not think there would be, convincing himself he was just being paranoid.

At that moment, a sensation of fear rushed through his body as he sat up in his seat shocked into an instant alert. His mind inexplicably shouted at him in what seemed like audible words, STAND UP! Terrifying thoughts overtook him as he pictured himself trapped next to the window with the two men between him and the aisle…. Then again it repeated in a strong commanding voice. DANIEL, STAND UP *NOW!* Instantaneous thoughts of how stupid it would look came to mind as he instinctively felt his legs bending upward until he was able to get one heel on the seat cushion. Then in one continuous motion, he grabbed the top of the seat in front, pulling himself upward while slipping his feet all the way under until he very quickly raised himself into the air, bumping his head against the overhead service panel. For a brief second, he had a glancing view above the entire cabin before he lost stability, falling further forward over the seat-back to see the older woman in front of him look upward. Feeling like the whole thing was an involuntary movement and extremely embarrassed with his face about four inches from hers, all he could think to say was, "Hello … sorry."

He pushed himself back, still half standing and humped over in an awkward position. He looked down at the shocked expression on Lance's face as his foot twisted and caught the blanket on Stefan's lap, pulling it a few inches to one side, exposing, to his horror, in a hyper-moment that progressed in slow motion, the plunger end of a syringe with Stefan's thumb at the end of it. If he had not moved at that precise moment, it would have been injected into his leg that had been inches away from him seconds before. The whole thing happened in one, long uncontrolled movement. He continued lifting one leg while swinging it over the two men, hovering above and straddling them for an instant before landing it firmly in the walkway with a loud THUMP. His other leg swiftly dragged across their laps, causing him to completely lose his footing and go careening toward the other side of the aisle.

The man in that seat saw what was happening, and in a reflexive action, put his hands up to protect himself as Daniel started to fall on top of him and pushed him backward, miraculously allowing Daniel to quickly regain his balance.

"You okay?" he asked.

"Yes, thanks … I'm so sorry, I apologize. Good reflexes."

"I'm surprised more people don't trip over each another in these tight spaces."

"I agree," Daniel said, trying to politely respond to the man who just helped him while keeping his body moving up the aisle and away from Lance, who was now unseen directly behind him, the whole episode happening within one very long stumble.

Daniel's heart was racing and he was feeling dizzy and sick as he gasped for air while backing toward the rear of the plane. Thankfully, he looked to the left and saw he was standing next to an unoccupied bathroom. Slipping in quickly, he locked the door behind him; another Bible verse came to mind. *The second woe is past; and, behold the third woe cometh quickly.*[11] He slumped down onto the toilet, resting his head on the wall behind him, just breathing and unable to think any intelligible

---

[11] **Revelation 11:14** The second woe is past; and, behold, the third woe cometh quickly.

thought for more than a minute as his breath started to return to normal and tears began to well in his eyes.

"Dear Lord Jesus," he prayed outloud, the sound of his voice muffled by the loud drone of the plane, "help me, please help me." He closed his eyes, squinting in mental anguish, then opened his eyes and for a split second saw three words scrawled on the wall in front of him. "Turn it around!" Then the words were gone. He reached his hand and weakly touched the wall a few inches in front of his knees.

As he sat there, a peace came over him,[12] and along with it, a sense of confidence and the knowledge of what he needed to do. Then his favorite verse in the Bible popped into his head. *I can do all things through Christ who strengthens me.*[13] Daniel must have repeated those words a thousand times since he received the Lord when he was twenty-seven, but never in his life did he think it would be tested in such a way.

Daniel took out his smartphone, and opening his Bible app, did a lookup on the words "fear not" and then pressed Isaiah 41:10–13. *"Fear thou not; for I am with thee: be not dismayed; for I am thy God: I will strengthen thee; yea, I will help thee; yea, I will uphold thee with the right hand of my righteousness. Behold, all they that were incensed against thee shall be ashamed and confounded: they shall be as nothing; and they that strive with thee shall perish. Thou shalt seek them, and shalt not find them, even them that contended with thee: they that war against thee shall be as nothing, and as a thing of nought. For I the Lord thy God will hold thy right hand, saying unto thee, Fear not; I will help thee."* Daniel smiled and pressed another link that took him to a familiar verse. Hebrews 13:6: *"So that we may boldly say, The Lord is my helper, and I will not fear what man shall do unto me."*

*This is where the rubber meets the road in trusting God,* he thought as he stood up and looked at himself in the mirror and turned on the water,

---

[12] **Philippians 4:7** And the peace of God, which passeth all understanding, shall keep your hearts and minds through Christ Jesus.

[13] **Philippians 4:13** I can do all things through Christ which strengtheneth me.

washing his hands and throwing some on his face. Then he spoke outloud to himself. "I will put ALL my trust in the Lord, no matter what happens."

Then he found himself almost smiling at the irony that he would remember his favorite sin. He never heard anyone say they had a favorite sin, but to him it was simply that. The sin of worry, *for whatsoever is not of faith is sin.*[14]

There had been a time when he thought that not worrying would be impossible, until once while trying to comfort a friend, he encouraged her not to worry. Instead of appreciating it, she had rebuked him. "Don't accuse me of worrying," she said emphatically. "I don't worry." That was the moment he knew it was possible to overcome that sin and he had been working on it ever since. But never in his wildest imagination did he think his faith would be tested with people wanting to kill him. *I choose to trust You Lord,* he prayed again. At that, he opened the door, walking directly into the turmoil that awaited him.

---

[14] **Romans 14:23** And he that doubteth is damned if he eat, because he eateth not of faith: for whatsoever is not of faith is sin.

# CHAPTER 11

*Turn it around,* he thought as he walked down the aisle and passed Lance, giving him a pat on the shoulder, then turning to look back at the two of them with renewed confidence. Remarkably, in the midst of all this, he still held his peace, confident the emotion was visible in his expression.

He could see the sales reps going to the meeting in Pisa sitting in one group, taking up the first three rows in Delta's Comfort Section. He searched until he saw Jim sitting in the second seat from the aisle. "Hey, Jim, will you and the rest of your CIA team be working on any covert operations while you are here in Italy?"

Jim laughed, turning to his associate sitting next to him, who was shaking his head and was the one who answered. "Do you know how many times I get asked if I am in the CIA?" he said, smiling. "Sometimes I just say yes then look them up and down and leave without telling them the truth …"

"Outstanding!" Daniel said excitedly. "You guys want to have some fun?"

"Why, what do ya got in mind?" asked Jim.

"I got to talking with the two dudes next to me and I am pretty sure they brought pot on the plane with them. They seem nervous about it …" he said, drawing it out, "and I thought it would be fun to …"

"I'm in," Jim interrupted. "What do you need me to do? Oh, and by the way, this is Joe, and Joe, this is Daniel." They both nodded. "He's on the way to Italy to look for a place to honeymoon this summer."

"Congratulations! And say goodbye to freedom while you're there ...," Joe said, making a wise crack. "I'm only kidding. I've been married for twelve years and I would do it again. I hope you are as fortunate."

"Thanks," Daniel said sincerely. "Anyway, to answer your question, nothing bad, I'm going to tell them you guys are with the CIA, the anti-drug trafficking unit on the way to a meeting in Pisa." He laughed. "I am sure they can see us talking ..." Daniel looked up the aisle and nodded to them. "So next time you pass our seats going to the restroom, just give them a once-over. I think their expressions will be priceless. Then don't say anything, I'll take it from there."

"All right. Sounds like something to make this boring flight a little more interesting. You will tell them the truth before they get off the plane, won't you?" asked Jim.

"Of course ... short of being a couple of hit men, I promise," he said, laughing. "You have my word. Scout's honor." Daniel held up three fingers.

"Holy cow, the guy was a Boy Scout, too," Joe said, and they all laughed.

"Thanks, this should be fun," Daniel said, addressing Jim. "I will try to catch up with you when we get off the plane and let you know what happened."

"Sounds good."

Daniel walked toward the back of the plane, passing Lance and Stefan without giving them a glance, searching for a place to sit until he had to return to his seat for breakfast and landing. He wished he could tell one of the hostesses what was going on, but he knew that would be a bad idea. Any problem on an international flight would create major scrutiny and it was doubtful that they would believe him. What would he say? "Excuse me, ma'am, the two guys sitting next to me are hit men. Can you please help me?" No, and if he was questioned by the authorities, he could not prove a thing. Assuming the two guys were pros, they would walk away scot-free and make him out to be a nut or the bad guy. What he needed now was to get off the plane and make it to Liz and Toni's … that was the objective.

The aircraft was packed and he could not find one empty seat in coach. The only possibility on the wide-body Airbus 330 was to sit on the floor in front of one of the emergency exits. Unfortunately, the older man who had entered the plane with his body guards was sitting in the aisle seat of that row, one of his men in the window seat and the other across the aisle from him.

*You have got to be kidding,* he thought. But being emotionally drained and exhausted, he didn't really care. He looked them all in the eye and sat on the floor with his back against the cabin wall next to the exit door.

At that moment, the flight attendant started to walk by, then stopped and turned to look at him with a questioning look on her face.

"I am sorry, I have a problem with the muscles in my legs and I need to keep them stretched out straight for a while if you don't mind," Daniel said apologetically.

"Well, I'm not supposed to, but there aren't any open rows where you could stretch out, so I'll look the other way this time," she said, adding, "But you will have to return to your seat in about fifteen minutes for breakfast and then our preparation for landing in Rome." Then she said jokingly, "I've got my eye on you, so behave yourself."

"Okay, I promise." Daniel smiled while leaning his head back and glancing out of the corner of his eye at the three men who were now staring at him, but had not said a word. Every muscle in his body was aching and the mental exhaustion was so strong that within a few minutes, although hard to believe, he had fallen asleep.

He jolted awake as breakfast was being announced in time to see Stefan exchanging a few words with the fat man before quickly moving past him. Daniel stood up a bit groggy then turned directly toward the three and said, "Buongiorno," with the friendliest voice and most congenial look he could fake. He then returned to his row. As he moved past Lance and Stefan, he purposely knocked against their knees and excused himself before taking his seat.

He looked out the window at the blue sky, then turned to them with a confident and almost playful sound in his voice. "This is a nice day for a flight, isn't it?" At that, he slapped Stefan on the leg in a friendly way to emphasize his point.

"You arrogant piss ant," he said with a snarl. "This isn't over."

"Oh, no?" Daniel said confidently. "I think it is. By the way, did you notice those guys I was talking with? You know the ones. I mean … I nodded to you while I was talking with them." He watched their expressions before continuing. "It turns out that they work for the CIA, and guess where they are going? Come on, you can do it. Come on, guess …," he goaded. "No? I'll tell you. They are on their way to Pisa to a conference. Same place as me … incredible coincidence, isn't it? Obviously, they cannot wear a pin on their lapel with their logo since they work for such a secret agency. I am sure they wouldn't admit it if you asked, but if you observe, they are all wearing red, white, and blue ties. Patriotic and a dead giveaway I would think. How about you?"

"Do you honestly think we are going to believe that, you scumbag?" he said, unconvinced.

"Not necessarily. We are Americans and free to believe whatever we want. As for me … I am hungry right now. How about you guys?" Daniel said, lowering his tray table as the hostesses were about to serve the morning meal before arrival at Leonardo de Vinci-Fiumicino Airport in Rome.

The three remained quiet while they finished their meals and their trays were removed. Then Daniel noticed Joe coming up the aisle. On his way to the restroom, he presumed. *Here we go,* Daniel thought.

As Joe walked by, Lance held out his hand, touching Joe lightly on the arm. He stopped and Lance said in an inquisitive and genial voice, "Hey, is it true you guys are with the CIA?"

"What business is it of yours?" he said, pausing. "Why … are you guys concealing anything? Maybe we should search you two." Joe said the words in an intimidating way while slowly giving both of them a scrutinizing once over. "I've got my eyes on you two." He then continued down the aisle without waiting for a response.

Daniel watched, hoping they would fall for it. For the first time in his life, he understood the difference between true faith and a faith that was only made up of words. In church he talked the talk, but never seriously walked the walk of faith. Much of his life had been that way until now. He was thankful that this time it had a depth like never before. He was EXPECTING the Lord to back up His Word, and BELIEVING in Him for his life. At the same time, it was clear that what he was seeing being played out in real life, would be veiled to others observing. How could there ever be a way for him to tell others what the Lord had done for him? Who would believe it? He thanked God and bowed his head with a smile on his face.

How in the world could it be a coincidence that he would meet Jim before boarding the plane and find out he worked for a company with the initials CIA? This meant that before he got onboard, the Lord knew this was going to happen and was actually preparing him for it. *Awesome ... Lord, you are awesome!* He turned the thought into prayer. And the words "Turn it around." He used those exact words with his team all the time when they were working through a difficult problem with a franchise owner. They were expected to use their own ingenuity to work it out to the best of their ability ... which they did most of the time. From their perspective, they were confident that he would back them up, regardless of what happened. When he heard those words, he knew exactly where they were coming from and what he had to do. It all boiled down to his own actions and faith. At that same instant, he received the marvelous sense of a peace that passed understanding.[15] A peace that happens in a situation that would be impossible to believe one's self, had they not personally experienced it ... like this one that only God could have orchestrated. *Wow, what a mighty God we serve! He thought.*

It was only about thirty minutes until landing. Looking out the window at the clouds passing by, Daniel began to see lots of homes and traffic below. "Hey, you guys, we must be over Italy now. I can see a city. I wonder which one it is."

---

[15] **Philippians 4:7** And the peace of God, which passeth all understanding, shall keep your hearts and minds through Christ Jesus.

"PISA!" Stefan said, turning toward him, bursting the name out contemptuously, stretching it out with a bone-chilling expression.

Daniel maintained his confident facial expression while another stab of fear assaulted him inwardly.

After landing, Daniel remained seated, wanting them to deplane before him. He watched Stefan and Lance entering the crowded aisle. Just before they began to move away, he said loudly, "It was nice to meet you two and congratulations on your wedding. You two make a nice couple." At that, the older lady who sat in the seat in front of him stood, turning with a disgusted look on her face while Daniel blew a kiss toward them. She first stared at Daniel then Stefan and finally Lance, giving them all a sour look before rolling her eyes and moving into the walkway behind them.

Wanting to avoid the fat man and his two bodyguards, he slipped into the row across from him and made his way to the further aisle while taking his time and stopping to thank the flight attendant for allowing him to sit on the floor, before entering the jetway that would lead him to the concourse.

He was very happy to see that it was jammed with travelers, and even happier to see Jim and Joe standing outside the men's room waiting for their associates. He walked up to them laughing.

"You, guys, it was priceless. You should have seen their reaction when you walked away, Joe."

"What did they do?" asked Jim.

"It must have scared Lance because he quickly reached into his pocket and then stuffed something in the seat-back pouch. Stefan didn't believe it at all. But it was a good try … and ya never know, the two of them may have skedaddled out of the airport already." The three laughed and talked as they made their way to baggage claim.

"Hey, ya know what? I decided I'm going to look for a place up in the Lombardy region which is the area surrounding Pisa. Do you think I could catch a ride with you guys?"

"I am not sure they will allow it, but I can check," Jim said. "One of the guys did not show up, so there should be room."

"No need," offered Joe. "The transportation company will be expecting twelve and we will have twelve."

"Good point," Jim said, nodding to Joe and then Daniel. "Just hang with us and no one will know the difference. We can tell them once we are on the way. And wait—" he reached into his carry-on, handing him an extra tie he brought, "Now you will look like one of us."

"Thanks, I really appreciate it."

The three made their way down to baggage claim, stopping at a booth along the way to exchange their dollars into euros. Daniel was especially glad to see his backpack as he had forgotten to grab his reading glasses out of it before leaving West Palm Beach. He flipped up the flap then remembered he stuck them in the outer pouch that was intended for a water bottle. While reaching in to pull them out, he felt a tiny round thing lying loose on the bottom. Thinking it was a piece of packaging, he removed it along with his glasses. It looked like a small, round battery, so he examined it more closely. Seeing two tiny holes on the other side, he quickly dropped it back in the pouch and joined his new friends.

They found the van waiting in a section with dozens of vehicles parked next to one another that looked exactly alike except for their markings. They all carried twelve passengers and were either for rental car companies, hotels, or chartered individually for small groups like the one they were on. They got in and tossed their bags in the storage area while introducing themselves. Daniel felt safe for the moment, but it was now a certain reality that it would not be permanent. As soon as he saw the little button, he guessed it was a transceiver communicating with someone and knew just getting off the plane and out of the airport was not going to be the end of it.

Jim and Joe introduced him to the guys and told them of his upcoming wedding and what he was up to. They teased him about getting married and welcomed him aboard. Now he was going to have to make an excuse to get off the bus.

"Oh man," Daniel said to Jim. "I can't go with you, guys. I told my cousins I would see them after I arrived." He acted as if he had legitimately forgotten. "It is a good thing I remembered or I would really be messed up." He apologized. "At least I am in the right place to catch one of these shuttles."

They understood and wished him the best. He had placed his backpack in the overhead storage area. When he reached up, he slipped his hand into the pouch, pulled out the button and flicked it toward the back of the shelf. He then pulled out a jacket and a cap that was inside. While reaching for it, he noticed there was a shuttle next to theirs going to the Hilton. Their door was open and only a few feet away from the driver in their own van. "Hey, you guys," he said, addressing the group. "I want to thank you all very much and I wish you the best. Oh, and Jim," he said removing his tie and handing it back to him. "Thanks for the loan and you have no idea how much I appreciated meeting you."

Daniel slipped off their bus with his head down, now wearing a blue jacket and cap and slipped onto the other van. To anyone watching, it would appear he had gotten on the wrong shuttle, which happened all the time.

# CHAPTER 12

After arriving at the Hilton, Daniel walked into the main lobby and then, without stopping, left out the side exit, returning to the front of the hotel again, opening the door of a taxi and getting into the back seat. "The American embassy, please," he said to the driver.

It was now completely dark yet Rome's center city was awash with lights, traffic, honking horns, and exuberant chaos. With all that was on his mind, he had not given much attention to the fact it was early December with Christmas approaching. Holiday lights garnished every business and street in downtown Rome, illuminating it with a dazzling array of delightful brilliance. Colorful holiday images lit up the busy thoroughfare below depicting angels blowing trumpets, holly, and stars. The taxi approached one park with a giant Christmas tree adorned with all the ornamentation one would expect, including the bright star at the top. Next to it, directly facing the approaching vehicles, was a semitransparent hologram of Jesus dressed in a gently blowing white robe, hovering about thirty feet above the traffic. His arms were opened wide and He was lovingly beckoning all to enter into His embrace.

"Do you know of a tourist area within walking distance of the embassy?" he asked the driver.

"Sì. My English no very good, but I talk little," he answered. "I take you to Piazza Barberini. You find there, Gli americani, no far ambasciata, you see Triton Fountain, okay?"

"Yes, grazie," Daniel said, using his limited Italian.

A few minutes later, the taxi pulled up in front of Peppy's Bar. Daniel paid the fare and thanked him again. He strolled to a side street looking for a hotel. Finding one, he walked into a cramped lobby and an oversized front desk. It looked like the proprietor was talking with a friend, both of their hands communicating as fast as their conversation. He had one room left which he took sight unseen, and within minutes opened the door to a small room with a bed and modest chair squeezed against a window overlooking the street. He dropped his backpack on the floor and fell to his knees against the side of the mattress as tears began to flow. Exhaustion had taken its toll; as he prayed, he lay his head on the bed. The next thing he remembered was waking up sore all over and climbing onto the mattress, pulling the bedspread over him. Then it was morning.

Daniel opened his eyes and could hear people talking in Italian from the street outside, along with a car applying its brakes and coming to a stop. He lay there not wanting to get up and face the day ahead. While on the plane, he thought it might be a good idea to go to the embassy and tell them what was going on. He knew they were not the right government agency to report something like this, but the fact he was out of the country at an American embassy might somehow give credence to his story, and at least it was worth a try.

He did not call Toni and Elisabetta before leaving the states and now wondered if he should have at least told them he was coming. But he hadn't taken any chances. If he had called from JFK or his uncles, they might not have been able to track the phone he was using, but they might be able to trace all calls to Italy during the same time frame and try to zero in on his location. If they could connect him to someone ... like family, they could learn the number and location of the burner phone it was coming from. That being the case, he would be toast and his cousin's family would be in danger. *No..., showing up unannounced is better all the way around and keeps them safe and uninvolved.*

He had not eaten since breakfast on the plane. He downed an espresso along with cold cuts and bread in the lobby before checking out.

The embassy was a straight shot down Via Vittorio Veneto three blocks away … he hoped. When he asked the portly lady at the front desk, she told him, "Guarda a destra quando le strade si uniscono," pointing while shaking her right hand in the air and then taking her left hand and bringing it toward her right one while making a humming sound and joining it with the palm of her right hand and laughing good-naturedly. "Down the street on the right where the streets merge," he repeated back to her in English. "Grazie"

It was a bit too cold out for the jacket he was wearing, *but at least it was sunny*. His heart almost stopped beating as he began to hear the sound of someone running toward him on the sidewalk from behind. He instantly assessed his surroundings as it steadily became louder and closer. He forced himself to continue walking at the same pace even though his brain was screaming at him to break into a run. He could see the embassy ahead, just like the woman said, and he was almost there. Suddenly a man dressed in a business suit flew past him on his left carrying a briefcase. He had no idea why the man was running, but if it was to see if he could be spooked, it worked.

His heartbeat was just about returning to normal as he walked into the embassy, grateful to see the two Marines guarding the entrance. There wasn't a line, so he was able to go right up to the window.

"I would like to speak with a consular representative," he said to the young lady.

"May I ask what it is regarding?" she inquired.

"It is a business matter and difficult to explain. But I am an American citizen and I would appreciate your help."

"Certainly," she said, pressing a button. A Marine approached her and she explained the request to him.

The soldier came through the door to the lobby and asked Daniel to please follow him. Before that moment, he had never understood the sense of home one feels when visiting an American embassy while in a foreign country, and realized that this was the first moment he felt safe since his conversation with Greg. The Marine led him into an office and asked him to take a seat and fill out a form asking for his name, address, passport number, and the reason for his visit. He looked at the form wondering how in the world he could try to explain why he was there in just a few paragraphs, but he did the best he could.

Finally, a well-dressed gentleman entered the room, taking a seat across from him. "How can I help you?" he asked.

"I uncovered some things about the heads of my company. I work for a franchise called POP's Office Supply. They are in California and I think they are trying to kill me," he blurted out, unable to control his words. "I work for a franchise. They killed several of the owners and I'm not the only one on their list. One of the sales guys is on the run, too."

"I see. By the way, my name is John," he said in a somewhat comforting tone. "I have heard of the company." He smiled, trying to relax him a bit. "But why did you come here? I don't think there is anything we can do to help you. We don't have anything to do with business relations. The embassy is primarily a source for Americans with problems while traveling on foreign soil."

"I know, you are right," he said, stumbling over his words a bit. "I'm not quite sure why I am here … exactly." Daniel felt embarrassed and nervous. "I thought it best to get out of the country to give myself time to think. I have a cousin who is an attorney that lives here in Rome."

"Well then, Daniel. May I call you Daniel?"

"Of course."

"I think he would be the best one to talk with. Do you have his address?"

"No, but I do have his phone number."

"Well then, why don't you give him a call?" he said, getting up and bringing a landline phone over to the table, setting it in front of him.

"Okay, good idea," Daniel said, exhaling sharply. "I am sorry, I know I must sound like an idiot."

"You sound distraught. I don't know what is going on, but I do think it would be a good idea to be with family right now. If he is an attorney, I think it would even make it a better move."

The consular officer listened to the conversation he was having with Elisabetta. From the way it sounded, her mother was visiting from England. His cousin would be home in a few hours and they would be looking forward to seeing him. He watched as Daniel wrote down the address, told her he was at the embassy, and would be there as soon as he could.

Daniel left after thanking John for his help and apologizing again, trying to explain that he wasn't usually like this. He left figuring the guy must have thought him a total nutjob. But he had shaken hands with him professionally before saying goodbye.

*That was a waste of time,* he thought as he hailed down a taxi in front of the embassy. By the time he arrived at his cousin's home, he was an emotional wreck again. He lost all the faith he had on the plane and was beginning to see the obstacles rather than the Lord helping him through each of them. Maybe this was all a lie and he was just having a breakdown. Or was it easier to consider himself having a breakdown than facing the sequence of coincidences he had experienced? He remembered his Christian mentor telling him one time that we must choose to believe God's Word and not go back and forth between the devil's lies to our mind and our own reasoning.

His mind was in such a tangle of theories trying to determine which were from the Lord and which from the enemy of his soul. As hard as he searched, it seemed the truth was evading him. He repeated the instruction in his mind, but this time more as a directive to himself. The choice was to put all his trust in the Lord. All of it … everything …, placing his confidence in Him blindly, not counting on his own self or his opinions or common sense, nor insight or his own conclusions … just believing the Lord was involved and not caring he might look ridiculous. Simply trusting that if the Lord was allowing him to go through this, there was a purpose known only to Him and it was unimportant that he understood. It was only important that he followed what he considered the right thing to do and knowing that right or wrong, the Lord knew what was going on.

*I wonder if my guardian angel was helping me on the plane.* The taxi turned off the road and entered an apartment complex, crossing a speed bump that caused the small bells hanging from the rearview mirror to jingle. He snapped back to the present wondering what exactly he was going to say to his cousin.

Elisabetta was ecstatic to see him again. He remembered her having a special way of making everyone feel welcome. She had come to Italy on vacation, met Toni, fell in love, got married, and now had two young daughters. Toni did not speak English well, but had visited England enough times to grasp a basic understanding. What he did not know, he knew Elisabetta could translate and it was clear she was a pretty sharp woman in her own right.

She had just introduced him to her mother when Toni walked in the door.

"Cugino. How are you?" asked Toni. "It is good to see you."

"Gratzie, it is good to see you too, but actually, I could use a little advice from an attorney. I am going through an unusual situation at work. I discussed it with Uncle Sprandy and he thought it would be a good idea for me to take a few days off and travel here to talk it over with you." he blurted out. "I hope you don't mind my coming without notice. By the way, he and Beulah send their love."

"Surely, you are welcome anytime and I will do my best to help. But first I shall make a special meal of spaghetti … Alfredo ala Toni," he said, smiling and handing several long loaves of bread to his wife. "First, we shall celebrate our having the privilege of entertaining English family and American family, yes?" He smiled again.

"Yes!" Daniel said, returning the smile. At the moment, Toni could not have said a more appropriate thing because it was family he needed. He met him only once before, but had been so impressed that he wished he could have grown up knowing him. If they had lived in the same vicinity, he was sure they would have been close friends.

Daniel sat in the kitchen with Toni, Elisabetta, and her mother, sipping red wine and watching him making the Alfredo sauce then removing long strands of steaming spaghetti and heaping them into large bowls, into which he ladled huge portions of the most delicious white sauce he had ever eaten … then there was the garlic bread.

When they finished, Toni said, "Now we can go talk and I thank you because you here and I not wash plates." At that, Elisabetta swirled a kitchen towel and swatted it at his back side. "Now you see abuse I get from my English woman," he said, walking over and giving her a kiss. From what he could tell, they still shared the same feelings toward each other that he remembered when meeting them years before.

They walked into Toni's study. He closed the door and took his seat behind a mahogany desk surrounded by shelves loaded with what looked like legal reference books. "Now tell me, what problem you at work have?" he asked with a sincere expression on his face.

Daniel tried to explain it as best he could and Toni tried as hard as he could to understand with his limited English. Finally, they both agreed it was best to ask Elisabetta to join them.

After listening to the entire story, Toni sat thinking for a minute while scribbling some notes and then looked up, talking directly to him, with Elisabetta translating if she thought it necessary.

"I must look at this only from a legal standpoint," he said professionally while fiddling with his pen. "I believe the story you have told me, but it would be very hard to prove any of it. As you said, there is not a law about mismanaging a company and it would be very difficult to produce enough valid evidence for them to make a judgment without any shadow of a doubt." He paused. "However, it is also clear that if they have gone to the extreme of having others killed, by professionals, it would appear there must be a lot of money at stake. So we need to follow the money. Who stands to profit and how does that happen?"

"That is where I am lost," Daniel said. "I have no idea what anyone would gain by causing all the franchise owners to lose their businesses and investors to lose money in their stocks. It just doesn't make sense."

"It does not make sense when we look at it that way, but let's examine what you told me a little closer. You said the company that purchased the franchise was huge with multi-international subsidiary businesses and investments, right?"

"Right."

"Well, let's say that they are large enough to purposely collapse a company in order to make money on another."

"Why would they do that?" Elisabetta asked Toni in Italian, wanting to know the answer to the question herself. "Yes, why would they do that?" Elisabetta repeated in English for Daniel's benefit.

"I am just guessing," Toni said, turning to his computer. "They are on the American Stock Exchange, right?"

"Yes, that is correct."

He entered in POP's Office Supply and came up with today's purchase rate. "I know you said that POP's is the world's largest office supply franchise, but who would you say would be the second largest?"

"I guess that would be Office 4U, I think."

"Do you know much about that company?"

"I have heard the president of our company talking about them and he seems to have respect for them. Although they are much smaller, they appear to be well run and doing a very good job for their franchise owners. I think they have pretty much followed POP's success formula. Why?"

Toni typed in their information and quickly pulled up their stock prices. "Mama mia," Toni said, not needing the words translated. "This may be the answer. Their stock prices are not even in the same league as POP's. Much lower priced."

"I don't understand your point," Daniel said with interest.

Elisabetta glanced at Daniel. "Me either."

"Let's say that a group comes in to your company with the purpose of making the stock collapse. They mismanage it and it comes tumbling down. Now let's say that the same company invested heavily in the stocks of their competitor, whose purchase price is much less, but appears to be on track to increasing their value anyway, based on the fact that they are already viewed as a viable up and comer. What do you think would happen?"

"Their price would go up … fast," Daniel said, comprehending the elaborate ruse that it would take to put something like that into motion. "If that is the case, it should be easy to prove and make them culpable!" Daniel said eagerly, waiting for Toni's response.

"Culpable?" he said. "It SHOULD make them guilty, but I doubt that you would ever be able to prove it."

"Why?" Daniel asked, perplexed.

"Because at that level, you would be talking about so many layers of subsidiaries and shell companies making the investments, that even if it was tracked back to the company that bought POP's, it would be close to impossible to prove they did it on purpose," Toni said, adding, "From what you say, you have no physical proof, only the prospectus."

"Well, no, that is not exactly correct," Daniel said, shaking his head. "I do have some conversations between the president and two of the vice presidents that incriminates them individually. It would ruin their reputations, but who knows, with good lawyers and a large company behind them willing to kill people, they might get off."

"True, but most likely they would do some jail time," he said continuing. "How did you get them?"

"There is one other person at the corporate headquarters that I trusted with this information. Once I heard Will so upset, I knew I had to find out more and I went into action. I knew we had to turn the situation around. I just needed to find out what was going on. With all the sophisticated digital systems we have, it wasn't too hard to set something up, but in truth at that point I had no idea what was going on and the value of what I do have."

"How trustworthy is the person you asked?" Elisabetta questioned.

"She is a good person and it is unlikely they would ever suspect her of anything. She is a computer whiz in a motorized wheelchair and she goes to the church I frequent when I am in California."

"What did she do?" Toni asked, wanting to know if it gave Daniel any legal advantage.

"I asked her to keep an eye on them and record any private meetings she thought might be of interest. She did exactly that. One time she even used a small spy cam." He laughed. "She is a pistol and I wouldn't want to be on her bad side. Anyway, when I first heard the audio, I did not know what I had until later on. The problem is that it would only incriminate the senior staff individually, and I doubt it would help the franchise owners, no." He shook his head, adding, "I would rather hold them aside and keep it as insurance. I am not sure why, but I don't think using them now would be worthwhile."

"I see your point, and as an attorney, I hate to say it, but I think you are right. As long as you have the recordings, you stay alive, but only if they know about them."

"So you are saying that you think I should tell them?"

"Absolutely, once they know and if they believe you, I doubt they will want you dead. In fact, they may not even want to tell the people they report to. I doubt they would care about the senior staff to want to keep them alive, and from their end they might even become allies in a sense, agreeing to let you alone. Who knows? Miracles do happen."

"But you do think they will get away with collapsing the company?"

"You keep asking the same question, Daniel. Yes, I do. And there is nothing you can do about it. Get it through your head, my cousin. Accept it and move forward with those thoughts. Plan from there."

"That is really hard for me to swallow. If I do, a lot of people get hurt."

"Listen, if they invested this much money and effort, I doubt they would do it unless they were certain of the outcome."

"So then, what can I do?"

"Well, first I suggest that you record your entire story, noting people's names, places, and all of the evidence you have accumulated and where it is located, the prospectus, agencies you contacted, and the names of the individuals, etc. You can use Elisabetta's computer … sì," he said, looking at Elisabetta, who nodded enthusiastically. "You can pull documents you need off the internet if they are public knowledge, and do all while you are here. Make an audio file in your own voice; take photos of everything you need and put it on a flash drive, here." He reached into his desk and handed several to Daniel. "Make several copies; that way if something were to happen to you …" He stopped. "Although I hope that is not the case … I mean I hope no bad thing happen to you … you understand cousin?

"Yes, I do."

"Me too," Elisabetta chimed in. "We want you to come back when this is all over so we can celebrate with you."

"Yes, of course, thanks. I have already weighed that possibility and I am cool with it." He paused, thinking deeply about Toni's assessment. "So all this was for nothing then. They will get away with it."

"Well, Daniel, no. I did not say there was nothing you could do," he said, allowing his hands to join the words coming out of his mouth and moving so fast that Elisabetta couldn't keep up. She was stuttering and stopping, trying to translate as fast as he was talking, until she finally gave up and said to Daniel: "I think I can explain. He said that you may not be able to stop the company from what they are doing, but you still have time to prepare and arm the franchise owners. He thinks that is the best you can do."

"You are in marketing, Daniel. Do your best to create your own campaign," Toni advised, while Elisabetta struggled to find the right words that would convey his thoughts. "Contact the most influential owners and explain to them all that has happened."

"Okay, then what?" Daniel asked, leaning forward and working hard to receive every word he was saying.

Toni shook both of his hands in front of him as if he really wanted to communicate his thought correctly. "First, you must get out of your head that you are going to be some kind of hero that is going to swoop in and save the day. That will not be the outcome. I think the best you can hope for is that you will give them the ammunition to fight their own battle. Then once you have done that, leave the company and get on with your own life."

Daniel lowered his head with a brooding expression on his face. "I do not care if I am a hero, but I do care that the franchise owners come out unscathed." He looked at Toni and then Elisabetta, feeling discouraged.

"What will you do now?" Toni asked.

"It's already Wednesday and my vacation is over on Monday. I think I will catch a plane back to JFK in the morning and visit my family in South Jersey over the weekend. I have a few owners on my schedule in New Jersey next week anyway." He paused while collecting his thoughts. Besides, I think I am safer being around the franchise owners.

"That sounds like a good idea. But if I were you, I would choose very carefully those you share information with."

"I agree. As it turns out, I had scheduled a visit with an owner in North Jersey next Tuesday who is the new president of POP's Franchise Owners Association. I think he will be the best one to tell. He is well respected and maybe we could even work out some kind of plan."

"Excellent!" Toni said. "Figure out your flight information. I will drop you off at the airport in the morning."

# CHAPTER 13

The following morning, Daniel said his goodbye to Elisabetta and her mother and was off to the airport by 7:30 a.m. He decided against making a reservation the night before, electing rather to time his trip to the terminal and call American Airlines exactly two hours before the flight. He was trusting the Lord to not be held on hold for an hour. *That would be a miracle,* he thought, smiling inwardly while whispering a silent thank-you ahead of time.

He had confirmed with the customer service representative that two hours would be acceptable *if* the reservation was made directly with them, while being cautioned that he would need to check in at the gate at least thirty minutes prior to departure in order to board the plane. He was also sure that as soon as he booked his ticket, he would be back on their radar. Knowing that, he placed the charge on his credit card aware that it wouldn't make any difference at this point as his passport would tell them exactly where he was anyway.

As soon as he had gotten in the car with Toni, the fear started again. He did his best to cover it up, but the closer they got to the airport, the stronger the emotion. By the time Toni dropped him off at American Airlines, it was full blown. He knew check-in for an international flight was usually three hours, but he was purposely cutting it close and now there was a little less than ninety minutes. If he missed the flight, he knew it would exponentially increase the danger.

He was clearly concerned about what would happen once he arrived in the USA, but the Bible instructed him to take one thing at a time.[16] He could only wonder how the Lord was going to protect him. But somehow, even that thought brought with it a sense of unholy terror.

Daniel gave his cousin the customary kiss on his left cheek then his right one, watched him get back in his car and drive away, taking with him his sense of safety. He waved until he disappeared out of sight, then turned, walking past the curbside check-in deciding to take his back-pack with him this time. As hoped for, everything went smoothly. He reached the gate just as they were boarding. Within minutes they had checked him in and he entered the enclosed boarding bridge.

The flight attendant was waiting to welcome him, and after checking his boarding pass, gestured toward the correct aisle to find his seat. As he began moving to the back of the plane, he was surprised to see so few passengers. He was standing between first class and coach as he entered the first section of coach, which was almost empty. He continued further back to his assigned seat at 36-C. This time he was on the aisle in the middle section, with four empty seats to his right with plenty of room to stretch out and take a needed nap on the way home. He listened to the doors being locked into place as the engines started to whine as they were turned on.

Then his worst nightmare materialized and brought with it another enormous stab of fear. He must have just made it onto the plane before they shut the door. The man was ... he searched for the right word ... bedraggled. His clothes were dirty and disheveled and his hair uncombed, with a greasy and unshaven face. He stopped when he got to his section, looking around the cabin. With most of the seats being empty, he wondered where he would end up sitting, hoping that it would be far away from him. As the thought crossed his mind, the guy spotted him

---

[16] **Jeremiah 17:7–8** Blessed is the man that trusteth in the Lord, and whose hope the Lord is. For he shall be as a tree planted by the waters, and that spreadeth out her roots by the river, and shall not see when heat cometh, but her leaf shall be green; and shall not be careful in the year of drought, neither shall cease from yielding fruit.

and walked closer. He was relieved when it seemed that he was going to continue walking past him, but began to tremble when he took the seat directly behind his.

They had not even taken off yet and it was a ten-hour flight. *Oh Lord,* he began praying, *this is too much. I'm telling you right now that I cannot handle this one. Please, don't expect me to. I know what I can handle and this is past that point. I promise you, I am telling you the truth, no more.* He pleaded as his eyes began welling up with tears. He became so agitated that he started squirming around completely unhinged in his seat. Suddenly, he stopped himself, forcing his body to remain still as he tried to regain control. The fear itself was like a fiery dart, the flame circulating violently throughout his body, spreading with it a sensation of dread. At the same time, his brain was trying to reach through the horrific thoughts. Even though he was ablaze with fear, he kept repeating to himself, *I am reacting … not acting, I am reacting … not acting.* After several minutes of repeating those words to himself, he found he was approaching the vicinity of faith.

By the time the hostess had come by with his first meal, his breathing had returned to normal, but it was like he had a third eyeball able to focus on the man in the seat behind him. He had been praying nonstop, working at getting back to a state of faith and reminding himself that anything less than faith is sin and sin is separation from God. Not what he wanted when he needed to be as close to Him as possible.[17] At the moment, it was hard getting that reality … to become reality.

Finally, he lifted the tray table into its upright position. He had calmed down, realizing the guy was probably some thug that had nothing to do with all of this and it was just his mind playing tricks again.

The section of the jetliner he was in only had about a dozen people scattered around the coach class seats. He was trying to figure out why he

---

[17] **Romans 14:23** And he that doubteth is damned if he eat, because he eateth not of faith: for whatsoever is not of faith is sin.

**Isaiah 59:1–2** Behold, the Lord's hand is not shortened, that it cannot save; neither his ear heavy, that it cannot hear: But your iniquities have separated between you and your God, and your sins have hid his face from you, that he will not hear.

had taken the seat behind him when the answer came with another fiery dart.[18]

It started with the cushion of his seat-back momentarily thrusting forward and returning to its normal position. At first it felt like a child was behind him pushing the back of his seat forward. The only thing missing was the giggle that followed and the apology from the parent while playfully scolding the little one. But this time it didn't stop.

"Excuse me," Daniel said, turning. "Would you mind not doing that?"

It continued and, again, Daniel could feel the fear welling up in his stomach. This time he stood up and turned toward the man with one knee on the seat cushion. "What is your problem?"

The man started speaking words in Italian that he did not understand, but he said them antagonistically. He sat back down in his seat unable to recover from the fear for almost thirty minutes.

Then he remembered the words the Lord told him. Somehow as that thought came, it brought with it confidence and faith and knew exactly what he had to do. *This is actually going to be fun,* he thought. *Lord, as I do this, would you please bring upon this man double the fear he brought upon me? Oh and Lord, I pray for his soul.*

Daniel stood and walked back several rows past him to go to the restroom. Upon returning, he placed both of his hands on the headrest of the seat the man was sitting in, pulling himself into the row and sitting directly behind him. He waited a few minutes, smiling and watching his hands move around on the armrest. He waited for about thirty seconds before inflicting the first thrust with his knee. After three or four more jabs into the back of the seat, he reached his hand between the opening at the top of the seats while pointing a finger at the unseen man's head until it came in contact with something very greasy, assuming it must have been an ear. He brought his hand back and wiped his finger repeatedly against the seat-back and instinctively brought it up to his nose and took a whiff, almost throwing up at the stench.

---

[18] **Ephesians 6:16** Above all, taking the shield of faith, wherewith ye shall be able to quench all the fiery darts of the wicked.

Finally, Daniel stood up and walked into the aisle, deciding it was time to confront the man. He realized it was unlikely he would understand a word he was saying, but if he didn't, he was going to make sure he understood his tone and gestures.

"Hey, dude, how you doing?" he said with a jovial sound in his voice. "You think you are scaring me but know this. I have friends in very high places. Much higher than the hoods you work for. My father has a limitless amount of money to track you down, bring misery to you, maybe even your family. If I were you, I would be thinking about my own death right now. Fact is, I am sure you're going to hell …, but then again you never know. God gives everyone a second chance. In fact, I will even pray for you, you disgusting sack of grunt." He drew out the last words, giving them a guttural sound, with a determined look on his face. Even if he did not understand one word, he would have gotten the implication from his tone of voice.

"I sorry, I no hurt you. No hurt my family," he begged.

*So he did understand English,* Daniel thought, returning to his seat. *How in the world would they even let a grease ball like that get on the plane?*

The rest of the flight was uneventful with the exception of the times he would occasionally stick his knee into the seat-back and once or twice reaching around the side of his seat to pat him on the arm, remembering not to take a whiff and frequently visiting the restroom to wash his hands.

He remained so focused on the man he realized that he rarely saw the flight attendant except when she brought the meals and took the tray away. She hardly had said more than a few words to either of them during the flight. Then the most astonishing thing happened after the plane landed in New York.

The male flight attendant asked everyone to remain seated once they arrived at the gate, as they had to recheck the passenger US customs entry forms, apologizing and informing them it would only be a brief delay.

Soon after that, he was surprised to hear the rear cabin door opening, as a rush of outside noise entered the plane along with the high-pitched sound of the engine winding down. With so few people, it didn't make sense for them to use two jet-walks to disembark. He turned in his seat to see four men rushing onto the plane, three of them wielding guns.

The man in front of him stood up in a panic and started to run toward the front of the plane just as two more men started moving up the aisle from that direction. He simply lifted his arms in the air, realizing the futility of trying to get away. He watched as the officers cuffed him and walked past exiting the rear passenger exit.

"Mr. Davidson," the officer said, flashing a badge, "would you please come with me?"

"Sure … do you know what that guy was doing to me? I was just giving him a taste of his own medicine … honest. He started it, honest. I'm the victim here," Daniel said.

"Just follow me."

Once they reached the jetway and were walking toward the concourse, they met another man dressed in a suit and tie who flashed an FBI badge at him.

"Mr. Davidson, I am Special Agent Doug Hensley with the FBI. We need you to come into the terminal and take a seat," he instructed in an authoritative tone, ushering him off the plane and into the gate area.

Daniel sat down in the empty waiting area, nervously watching the now-handcuffed man being loaded into a golf cart-like vehicle and carted away through the busy international arrival concourse. Man being loaded into a golf cart-like vehicle and carted away through the busy international arrival concourse. Three other men in jackets and ties approached with their hands extended. He stood and shook their hands as they introduced themselves as FBI agents while escorting him back onto the jetway. They exited at the side door, just before reaching the aircraft cabin entrance.

He moved carefully down the narrow stairway to the tarmac, where there was a car waiting for him. Once he got in, it drove away from the gates and entered a side rode next to an active runway, stopping as a Boeing 747 crawled its way to positioning itself on the take-off runway. The car then continued to an adjacent airport hangar where they came to a stop beside an entrance with a sign indicating that it was airport operations.

They directed him into the building then to a conference room and asked him to wait. A few minutes later, the FBI agent he met on the plane came and took a seat across from him. "Hi, Mr. Davidson. Again I am special Agent Doug Hensley. May I call you Daniel?"

"Of course. What is all this about?"

"Let me give you a recap. You arrived in Rome two days ago and visited the American embassy with a business problem. You were told they could not help. The consular you met with, however, thought you were sincere and decided to follow up with the Military Intelligence and Security Service, which is the Italian equivalent to our CIA. It turns out one of the people on the plane that arrived with you was a man notable to them and traveling with four of his associates, so they decided to contact the CIA and keep an eye on you. Are you with me so far?"

"Yes."

"They were able to confirm that you were visiting an attorney cousin as you said." He scanned his notes. "This morning you checked in at the last minute and, with a little help from our guys, were able to make the flight. Then right before the plane left, the man you saw in handcuffs, his name is Piero … something." He flipped through his notes, looking for his last name, then determining it non-essential information, he continued. "Anyway, he snuck on without a passport. When they ran facial recognition, they found he was a low-level hit man that could be traced to the same individual who arrived on the same flight as you." He paused. "This is where we came in. Naturally, the airline has a sky marshal onboard and he was monitoring everything on his smartphone as he had been patched in to the same live shots we were viewing. He was ready to step in had it escalated and you were in danger. But that didn't happen."

"Thank God for that," Daniel said.

"Well, at least you know we were watching," he said, smiling. "I have to tell you from what I heard, you had a number of agents coming in to view the monitor during your altercation with Piero. I was told that when you stood up, took a seat behind him, and started punching his seat that the agents were cheering you on!"

"Why would he do that?" Daniel asked. "I mean, if he was there to kill me, why wouldn't he have kept a low profile?"

"I think it was just the intimidation of a low-level goon on the totem pole. If he had been successful, he would have had a story to tell and moved up the chain. We found a hard plastic knife on him in a sheath in his pocket. He would probably have put it together right before getting off the plane and slipped it into your heart, leaving you dead on the plane while he quickly got off and disappeared."

"Are you serious?" Daniel was shaking his head, with fear coming across his face again.

"Sorry, I should not have put it that way, but the truth is, you should be thankful you are still alive. Anyway, are you with me so far?"

"With you … absolutely … and I feel like I am reliving it!" He continued, "Do you have any idea how terrified I was … on both of those flights? I have never been so scared in my life."

"But you handled it well, especially after escaping the guy with the needle on the first flight," he said, sitting back in his chair and relaxing a bit. "It is a rare occasion for us to see someone outside of our profession handle themselves like you did. You knew how to think on your feet and adjust your thinking according to the situation. The fact you were able to walk off the plane in Rome alive is a testament to your ingenuity."

"Thanks, but I am telling you for certain I was scared."

"Are you saying you don't think our agents get scared? Any day of the week they could be killed, but somehow they find the courage they need and that courage is usually driven by purpose. Theirs is to protect and serve." He paused, then asked the question that all this had been leading up to: "What is yours?"

"You mean, other than staying alive?" he said, not fully understanding his point.

"Yes, that is exactly what I am asking. What is your reason?"

Daniel had to think for a few seconds before answering. "I work for an incredibly good company. The man who started it drummed integrity into all of the employees. When I realized what was going on, I knew that every one of our franchise owners would be hurt. So I guess I wanted to protect them."

"Well, that's exactly what I wanted to hear." He sat back up, drumming the end of a pen on the table. "I am from our Washington, D.C., office and work business-related problems … in this case, with the Security Exchange Commission. To make it short, they oversee trading to prevent fraud and intentional deception to protect investors in the stock market. I was contacted because we think this may involve a company we have been watching. We were hoping that you might be able to be of service to us."

"Wait, I am not the one that uncovered the problem, if that is what you think. There are two of us and I assure you it is Greg who is the sharp one."

"Really, who is Greg? Tell me how the two of you got involved."

Daniel told him Greg was badgering him about the senior staff, then showed him the company prospectus proving that the new president and several of the men he brought with him had worked for companies that went Chapter Eleven bankruptcy, giving them protection from creditors; how the franchise owners at the meeting started dying; finally, how he and Greg decided to run for it until they could figure out what was going on; and about the burner phone they both had to use in emergencies.

Special Agent Hensley indicated to several other agents on the other side of the glass to join them in the interrogation room and asked Daniel to call Greg so they could bring him into their conversation.

Daniel reached into his backpack, pulled out the small cell, and dialed Greg, placing the call on speaker phone and listened to it ring.

The phone connected. "Daniel, is that you?"

"Yes, it's me, Greg. How are you doing? Are you all right?"

"Yes, I am, but Daniel, I think this is much bigger than we thought."

"I know you were right about everything. Look, I am with the FBI in New York."

"What … are you serious? What happened?"

"Greg, this is Special Agent Doug Hensley and with me are several other agents. We believe Daniel's story and think you are in danger, too. If you tell us where you are, we will send someone to pick you up."

Greg was silent on the other end of the phone.

"Greg, are you there?" asked Daniel.

"How do we know you are going to help us?" Greg asked.

The agents were surprised at his response. "Greg," said Agent Hensley, "I work with a team that investigates illegal business activities and I assure you that we are on your side."

"I believe him, Greg. I am with the good guys in their offices at JFK."

"Okay, as long as you are sure." Greg paused. "JFK?" Greg said. "I'm in Washington, D.C. I had a meeting today with a guy at the Federal Trade Commission."

"Greg, who did you meet there?" asked one of the agents.

"A guy by the name of Jim Foley, but he was a total waste of time."

"Who else was in your meeting?" asked Agent Hensley.

"Just him and I could tell he did not believe me. I saw him about twenty minutes ago."

"Where are you now?"

"I'm on a street walking toward the Metro."

"Can you see a police officer?"

"Wait a minute," he said, turning around in a circle. "Yes, I see one not far away."

"Okay, Greg, I want you to go over to the officer now and hand your phone to him. I will wait and, Greg, don't run, just act normal. It will be okay."

Greg walked to the officer. "Hi, I have an FBI agent on the phone and he wants to speak with you."

The officer gave him a questioning look as he took the phone. "Hello?"

"Hello, my name is Special Agent Doug Hensley with the FBI. Do you have your car nearby?"

"Yes, it's right here."

"Good. The man you are with could be in danger and I would like you to put him in your car, call for back-up just in case, and get him over to FBI headquarters on Pennsylvania Avenue. Do you know where it is?"

"Of course. It is only a few blocks away."

"Escort him into the lobby and we will take it from there. I will give them a call and they will be expecting you. Thanks for your help. Please give the phone back to Greg."

"No problem," he said, moving one hand to his holster and watching the surrounding area as he motioned for Greg to get in the car.

"Greg, this is Agent Hensley again. The officer will take you to FBI headquarters. Wait there. Your friend and I will catch a plane and meet you as soon as we can."

"Sure. Daniel, I will see you soon. It looks like we have a lot to talk about."

"You're not kidding! I had people trying to kill me but … God protected me."

Daniel could hear him take in a sharp breath. DANIEL, NOT NOW!

# CHAPTER 14

Daniel was waiting in the conference room at the FBI headquarters when Greg arrived. He jumped up rushing to his friend with his hand outstretched.

"I can't tell you how good it is to see you." Happy to see him still alive. "I can only wonder if what you went through was as scary. When this is all over, we need to go and grab a cup of coffee at Starbucks and talk about it."

Without skipping a beat, Greg said, "Nothing serious. I just went to a cabin at Lake Arrowhead and hid out for a couple of days to gather my thoughts and make a plan."

"I'm glad to see you made it through. So you remained at the cabin until when?" Agent Hensley asked.

"Until I decided the best place for me to get someone's attention that might be able to help would be in Washington, D.C., so I drove here," Greg responded.

"Did you talk to anyone in person or on the phone?"

"Not really. I was laying low trying to figure out what to do." Greg nodded at Daniel.

"Where exactly is this cabin you stayed at in Lake Arrowhead?" asked Agent Hensley.

"It's not really in Lake Arrowhead. It is in an area adjacent to it called Cedar Glen. I rented one next to the little store on the main road … Hook Creek Road, I think. I only went to the market next door to get food and stayed there until deciding to make the cross-country drive. I figured it is harder to hit a moving target," Greg said, moving around uncomfortably in his chair.

"Okay, good. Can we have your phone?"

"My phone? No, I'm sorry. Daniel and I decided we would use it once to call each other if necessary and promised to trash it. I tossed it in the Potomac River after our conversation, just in case someone had been able to track it."

"No one would have been able to track you on a burner phone …, but okay," said Agent Hensley. "You did the right thing and we are glad you are here and safe. We've got your back now."

"Are you sure neither of you have any proof?"

"Well," hesitated Daniel, "I do have some valuable recordings, but before you ask, the answer is no. I will not give them up yet."

"It is not a good idea to withhold anything from us. We are the ones trying to help you."

"Well, I don't have access to them right now anyway. When I think the time is right, I will give them to you. Let's leave it at that," Daniel said sternly.

"Okay, for the time being. But we will need them," he said flatly and clearly irritated, but unable to do anything and not wanting to press the issue at the moment.

The three talked for about an hour and a half. Agent Hensley explained there was no way they could prove anything without evidence and asked if they would be willing to take a quantified risk. They both wanted to know if it would help the franchise owners and were told it would, if they were successful, so they both agreed. The plan was to use them as targets to draw out another hit man. The FBI would be there to catch him or her, and hopefully, along with the man they already had taken into custody, could get both of them to plea bargain for a lesser offense if they gave them information that could incriminate the kingpin. Agent Hensley made it clear it was not a guaranteed plan, as these types were layered with protection, but it offered a good shot. After the discussion, they agreed to go with it. Daniel and Greg would leave the FBI headquarters, catch a flight from Philadelphia International Airport to West Palm Beach, where they would return to Daniel's home and be under close surveillance. BWI, Baltimore Washington International Airport, would be closer, but if anyone knew they had been taken to the FBI headquarters in D.C., BWI would be the most likely airport they would be checking.

They would be driven in an unmarked car to Philadelphia International Airport, about a two and a half hour ride, making sure they were not being followed. Tickets would be waiting for them in different names along with the appropriate IDs so that they could check in without fear of being tracked. That would get them back to Florida safely. They were told the real danger would be after they arrived at Daniel's home.

Agent Hensley accompanied them to the FBI receiving area, where they were placed in the back of a windowless restaurant delivery van. There were no seats so they had to sit on the floor. He wished them luck, telling them he would be watching. The two listened as the sliding door closed, and they observed the agent starting to walk around to get in the driver's side.

"Greg, don't say a word about anything. I don't trust Hensley."

"I know. I have information too and I think you are right."

Daniel gave him a look of surprise as the agent got into the van. They drove to the alley behind a Chinese restaurant about three blocks away where they were transferred into another van. This one was white and unmarked, with darkly tinted windows and two rows of seats in the back. Both took their own row and lay down in order to keep out of sight from anyone seeing them through the windows, but mostly so they could close their eyes and rest.

A little more than two hours later, they sat up and began to see overhead signs indicating they were entering the airport. Daniel had been praying the entire time asking the Lord for the next step. At that moment, he found himself thinking of his favorite Christian author, Corrie Ten Boom. Her father asked her one time as a child when they went to Amsterdam when he would give her the train ticket. Her answer was just before getting on the train. He told her that our wise Heavenly Father knows when we're going to need things, then warning her to never run out ahead of Him and that she would be given what she needed just in time.[19]

The driver followed the road toward American Airlines departures, as Daniel sat up noticing a school bus traveling next to them taking the turn toward arrivals. He smiled inwardly, thanking the Lord. The driver wished them well and reminded them that the FBI had their back. Daniel slid the panel door closed. They went directly to the ticket counter and, after showing their IDs, were given boarding passes, told they needed to proceed to the security area, were informed their flight was on time and would leave in about two hours.

"How about a cup of coffee, Daniel?"

"No, not right now," he said, picking up his pace, indicating he wanted Greg to follow. "Greg, you know how I am always telling you that God is a God of miracles?"

Greg halted angrily, forcing Daniel to stop and turn toward him. "Look, Daniel, I am stressed to the max and the last thing I need right now is one of your sermons ... so SHUT UP!" He said it a little too loudly, causing others to turn toward them and catching the attention of a security guard standing by an entrance. He immediately calmed himself, apologized, and the two started walking side by side again.

"Greg, I really am sorry to get you so upset. Honestly, I don't mean to. It is a bad habit. I do the same thing to my sister."

"You have a sister? I didn't know that."

"Yes ... a brother, too. I even have a mother and father."

"Funny."

"Do you get on their nerves as much as you do me and your sister?"

"More," he confessed. "But we are family and always there for each other."

---

[19] (Excerpt from 'The Hiding Place' by Corrie Ten Boom)

"And this is important to mention right now … why?" he asked sarcastically.

"Well, I am not positive, but I think the Lord is letting us know what to do now. Follow me," he said, walking down a flight of steps and then out the door in the arrival area spotting what he was looking for.

"You really are going to drive me crazy … you know that, don't you? Are you sure you know what you're doing? How can I even ask that question? Here I am following the guy who brings me to the FBI HEADQUARTERS in Washington D.C., to literally walk into some kind of trap you haven't even told me about yet. Do you think I am a total moron, Daniel?" They stopped again in front of a school bus with the name Cape May Christian School on the side. "Oh brother!" he said, looking at the name and guessing what was coming next.

"Greg, please calm down and follow my cue. I really do know what I'm doing, I promise," he said, entering the bus that was already loaded with students and getting the attention of the teacher.

"Hi, my name is Daniel Davidson. Is Jill Stake on this trip with you by any chance?"

"Jill? No, she didn't come this time. Do you know her?"

"Yes, she's my sister."

"Oh yes, I recognize you. I think she introduced us a few years ago when she gave you a tour of the school. Are you on your way to see her?"

"As a matter of fact, we are," he said, turning. "This is my friend Greg." They nodded.

"I'm Frances," she said. "I am the band teacher. We are returning from Florida where we won the band competition." She said it loudly, turning to face the students. At that they all let out a cheer and began laughing and talking again.

"We just arrived and when I saw the name on the side of the school bus, I thought it was some kind of God thing that you just happened to be here."

"Well, maybe it was," she said, quickly grabbing her cell phone from off the seat and speed-dialing Jill. "Hey, Jill, you'll never believe who we ran into. Hold on...." She passed the phone to Daniel.

"Hey, sis ... would you like some company?"

Frances and Greg spoke as Daniel was talking and refocused on him as he said goodbye.

"Your friend just said you were going to take a bus to Cape May. You might as well come along with us. What do you say, gang?" she said loudly.

The reply was loud and raucous, but Greg and Daniel certainly knew they were welcome. Some of the band brought out their guitars and the kids started singing songs. At one point, Daniel and Greg stood up in the aisle and started dancing, which sent the laughter and hoot calls to a very high decibel.

"You two aren't bad dancers for old guys!" yelled one of the students.

At that Daniel turned to face the rows from the front of the bus with both hands on his hips and a grotesque look on his face and sticking out his tongue. Greg pointed to him and then put his hands on his own hips contorted his own face, which sent the entire bus, including the teacher and bus driver, into uproarious laughter.

By the time they reached the parking lot of the school, even the kids were worn out. Frances let them exit first. Jill was waiting for them with a big smile on her face.

"Hey, brother," she said, walking up to him and wrapping her arms around him. "What a nice surprise. I brought two others along with me." Both of her sons, Troy and Clay, came running out from behind the car where they had been hiding and slammed into their uncle's waiting arms, knocking him backward onto the ground.

All the kids were laughing as well as Jill and Frances. Daniel stood up and turned to the two boys. "You two just wait. Keep your eyes open tonight because I might crawl into your bedroom and scare you to death," he said, raising his hands, making monster sounds, then pulling them both close and hugging them.

"So, Daniel, this is an unexpected surprise. What's up?"

Daniel looked at Greg who had been admiring the lightheartedness and answered. "Jill, this is my friend Greg. He is the National Sales Manager for POP's. We have a serious problem and need your help."

"Okay, then…, you two came to the right place. But not in front of the kids. Hop in the car and we will talk when we get home." Daniel smiled as he watched her place her hand on Greg's shoulder rather than his as they began walking.

They stopped for pizza on the way, which made the kids very happy, especially Clay who was the pizza monster of the family. When they got to Jill's home, she put the kids to bed and heated the three of them some hot chocolate. After passing it around and sitting in her comfortable chair, then pulling her legs underneath herself, she asked, "What's up?"

At that, they all heard Troy's voice from his bedroom call out, "Are you guys having hot chocolate?"

Jill said, "Go to sleep." That was followed by silence.

# CHAPTER 15

Daniel told her the whole story including what happened on the plane to and from Rome, while Greg filled in the gaps on his end.

"Daniel, I want to know what happed to change your mind about Hensley, and why did you give him my phone number in the first place?"

"I'm really sorry about that. I didn't put it together until after we had spoken," Daniel said trying to recount the series of events accurately and in order. "When Hensley picked me up at JFK, he said the FBI was notified by the CIA after their Italian equivalent had found that some mafia boss, or at least someone on their bad guy list, had been on the same plane as me going to Rome, and it agreed with what I told the guy at the American embassy. That is several layers of information being passed from one agency to another, and the only thing they had in writing from me was my short account of events I made on a small form while at the embassy. When Hensley was talking, he said he was impressed that I held my ground, even after they tried shooting me with a needle. The thing is that when I wrote the information on the embassy form, I did not mention the needle. That part just sounded so unbelievable and paranoid that I left it out."

"Okay, I understand. Good catch. Now it is my turn to fill you in on some information. This is the first moment we have had that I can tell you what was going on from my end," Greg said, pausing for a moment and leaning forward in his chair while rubbing his hands together. "I went into hiding at a cabin in Lake Arrowhead, California. I have been going to the same place for years and have a friend who lives within walking distance and is a full-time resident." He paused. "Lake Arrowhead is a small mountaintop community not far from Los Angeles," he said, looking at Jill. "I thought it would be a good idea to call the FTC. That stands for the Federal Trade Commission. They are a branch of the government that protects consumers from bad business practices. I thought I would fill them in and see what they would advise. Rather than call from there on my burner phone, I went down the mountain to the Riverside library and called them from another prepaid phone I bought in case I needed it.

"Anyway, I got hold of this guy who seemed very interested but said it would be better if we could meet and discuss it in person. He asked where I was and I lied and told him I was in the vicinity, but busy for the next few days. I offered to see him." He paused, looking at his watch. "Today actually, this afternoon … the truth is I wasn't getting much done in California, so I thought I would make the trip here."

"What was the name of the guy you were to meet with?" Daniel asked.

"Jim Foley," Greg answered. "Why?"

"I'm not sure. But if Hensley is in the FBI and is crooked, I wonder if the guy you were to meet with is, too."

"Okay, you guys," Jill said. "I think there is a little paranoia going on." I get the picture of the guy in the FBI … sort of, but not everyone in the United States government is a crook."

"You're absolutely right, Jill," Daniel said, "but there is no telling how deep this all goes and we're not taking any chances right now. Besides, you know how it says in the Bible that we are to only trust God and not put our trust in man?"[20]

"Oh, here we go …" said Greg.

"Yes," Jill said, ignoring the comment, "but that does not mean we are to think everyone is the enemy. That is simply just not the case. There are some good people in the world, you know."

---

[20] **Psalm 118:8** It is better to trust in the Lord than to put confidence in man.

"True, but to be honest, I don't know who to trust at the moment." Daniel sat back in his chair. "You wouldn't believe how clear God's leading has been so far. I mean, just like the bus at the airport. That was no coincidence."

"Yea, I agree, and He brought you right here to your big sister because He knows I will give you wise counsel."

"Oh brother!" Daniel said, rolling his eyes and smiling at Greg.

"Go ahead, make fun. But this is what I think," she said seriously. "The Bible also says where there is no counsel, the people fall: but in the multitude of counselors there is safety.[21] I think we should get Ted and Dad down here to see what they think."

"I like that idea," Daniel said, smiling and looking at Greg.

"Who is Ted?"

"He is our big brother. You will like him …, everybody does. Jill and I love one another, but we both love him the most, he's special, you'll see. He was our protector growing up. Oh, and Greg, you both have something in common. He is full of bologna just like you."

"I don't get it. And why is that, may I ask?"

"He is in sales."

"That one is lame even for you, dipstick," Greg said with a moan.

Jill laughed. "I'm staying out of this one. Let me get on the phone with him now and I will ask him to bring Dad tomorrow morning. I'll tell him I have a problem that needs fixing right away. Should I suggest they bring Mom?"

"Absolutely," Daniel said.

"Okay, you two get some sleep. Greg, the boys are bunking together. You are welcome to sleep in Troy's bed if you can stand the mess of a ten-year-old, and Daniel, you sleep on the sofa. Don't be surprised if a seven-year-old tackles you awake in the morning. I am going to bed. Good night." She abruptly disappeared down the hall.

"She seems like a good sister," Greg commented.

---

[21] **Proverbs 11:14** Where no counsel is, the people fall: but in the multitude of counselors there is safety.

"The best. She is bossy, but she is my big sister and that goes with the territory, at least that's what she tells me, but she is often right … as much as I hate to admit it."

"Understood. I have a big sister, too. Sometimes I want to throw her under a truck, but I wouldn't trade her for anything."

Daniel laughed. "Good night, Greg. And don't forget to say your prayers."

"I wasn't born with enough middle fingers to let you know how I really feel about you. And good night!" Greg stopped and turned before heading off to the bedroom. "You know, I do understand that the school bus being in the right spot at the right time was not a coincidence."

"Good. God loves you, too, Greg."

He started off down the hallway, then stopped and turned again. "I have a question. If I did become a believer, would I start sounding like you? I mean, is that part of the whole thing?"

"Greg, my friend … you would be worse … you're in sales."

Greg rolled his eyes. "You're the reason the gene pool needs a lifeguard. See you in the morning."

Daniel woke up abruptly at 6:45 a.m. with the weight of seven-year-old Clay landing squarely on his stomach and ten-year-old Troy jumping on his legs and holding them down while tickling his feet. After regaining his breath and stifling the urge to throttle the two of them, he started yelling to his sister. "Help! Help! Jill, I am being accosted by two little people. Quick … call the police!"

Jill stuck her head out from the kitchen where she was making a batch of French toast. "Sorry, bro, you're on your own. I'm busy fixing breakfast. Coffee is ready when you are."

Greg made his way into the kitchen rubbing his eyes. "That's the first good night's sleep I have had for a while."

Jill and Daniel looked at him with understanding, not saying a word. They all took turns in the bathroom while trying to gobble down the French toast before the kids could demolish the entire stack. Before long the kids were besieging Greg and he was feeling very much at home.

By eight, the doorbell rang and in walked Ted, then his beautiful wife, Joan, followed by grandma Jo and grandpa Marty, dressed in his customary khaki shirt and pants, mid-calf rubber boots, topped off with his signature bolo tie. Their arrival was followed by tight embraces and kisses, then introductions and finally Ted giving his sister a big hug while reaching over and pinching Daniel on the butt so hard that it forced him to raise up on his toes. He yelled out in pain while the entire family began laughing, having witnessed the same scene hundreds of times before.

"Now you know where my nephews get it from," Daniel said, addressing Greg. Then turning to Ted, he said, "You are going to get yours, Theo … and when you least expect it!"

They talked for a while and finally Joan told the kids to get their shoes on because she was taking them out for a few hours. The boys started to complain that they wanted to stay. She told them they could stay if they wanted, but they would miss out on a trip to the Cape May Zoo.

"The zoo?" said Troy.

"The zoo!" shrieked Clay happily.

They all watched as the two ran into their rooms, grabbed their sneakers, and ran out the front door while awkwardly trying to get them on their feet. Joan walked out after them and then said before closing the door, "And you two think you need prayer?" Then the room went quiet for a minute while everyone considered why they had come.

Marty was the first to speak. "It sounds like the two of you have gotten yourselves into some trouble. Jill told us a bit about it, but why don't you give us the whole story? We are here to listen and help. Before we leave, you will have a concrete plan."

"My dad is big on plans," Daniel said to Greg.

"Not just your dad," said Jo. "We want the two of you safe and are going to sit here until we have a firm plan and have asked the Lord for His blessing on it. Come on now, let's hear what you have to say."

Greg filled them in on the meeting at the Conclave in Atlantic City, how people started dying, and about the prospectus outlining the senior staff having come from companies that had filed bankruptcy. Then Daniel filled them in on the flight to Rome, leaving out the part about the two guys trying to kill him, not wanting to scare his mother any further; the embassy; the flight home, telling them the sense he felt the Lord telling him to turn the situation around. How he got behind the guy and started punching his seat-back as he had been doing to him, at which they all laughed and agreed it sounded exactly like something Ted would do. Then the visit to the FBI headquarters and the sense they both had to not trust the agent and letting them know that, at the moment, they were probably on the FBI's most wanted list, as they would be looking for them since they had not gotten on the plane to West Palm Beach as expected.

"Okay, Daniel," Ted started off. "You said it is doubtful that you will be able to prove collusion by the companies involved, and IF there were people getting paid off in government agencies to look the other way, that it would be almost impossible to prove. So then, what do you hope to do?"

"Good question. I hope to give the owners a fighting chance. Let me run it by all of you. Assume for the moment that there is nothing I can do to stop them from collapsing POP's Office Supply. Toni said the only thing left is to alert the owners so they have warning and can protect themselves. The new president of POP's Franchise Owners Association has a store in Paramus, New Jersey. I think Greg and I need to get to him and let him know what we think. If we show up together, unannounced, I think there is a good chance he would believe us. Especially when we show him the prospectus. I would bet anything he hasn't seen it."

"Son, that is an excellent idea," Marty nodded, agreeing. "You need to let them know and then you need to get out of it somehow."

"I may have taken care of that, too. When I visited Toni in Rome, he told me to make several copies of a flash drive with all the facts and a recording where I am telling the story in my own voice. I am going to hide it, along with photos of paperwork in several places along with all the other information. I already started doing that … and here, Dad," he said, handing him a memory stick. "This is one of the copies. Would you put this in your safe?"

"Of course, but how about the paperwork and the tape?"

"It's all there," Daniel said.

"Here?" he asked, examining the small electronic data device for a moment. "How is that possible?" He scoffed, then stuck it in his pocket without asking for an explanation.

"Yes, but in addition to that, you need to write it all out in … what do you call it when you send information out to people in a fax?" asked Jo.

"I think you are referring to a news release," offered Greg. "That is an excellent idea, and we can ask Sloan to email it to the other owners. He will have all their email addresses."

"Is email faster than a fax?" Jo asked.

"Slightly, Mom," Daniel said, giving her a loving pat on the back of her hand.

"Okay, but how are you going to get to Paramus?" she said with a concerned expression.

"I think I got that covered." Jill was considering her words while speaking. "Assuming the FBI is looking for you, the chances are they will be watching all of us if they haven't already. I can ask Frances, the teacher you met on the bus, if she will loan me her car. I will ask her to watch the kids on Monday and I will drive you there. Until then you can stay in my neighbor's home next door. They are seasonal and have a basement where you can stay tonight and tomorrow night. Just make sure you don't keep any lights on upstairs. I will keep my truck parked in their garage until Monday and get it when I take the kids to school. It's a good thing Hal installed the truck bed cover on the back. You guys can slip under it and transfer to her car when we get to school. She is a good friend and I am sure she will loan me her Ford Transit. Just make sure the kids don't know you are around."

"Jill, I don't know what I would do without you."

"Yeah, well …, keep thinking on that. You're gonna owe me. Let's see, how about round-trip tickets for me and the kids for a week at your home on the lake?"

"Deal," he said, appreciating her offer. "But I'm not sure I want you to take us. It could be dangerous."

"Why? I would be less likely than Ted and I wouldn't be in my own car. If they were tracking mine, they would find it at the parking lot at school and I will be back before the kids get out."

"I agree," said Jo. "It is dangerous, no doubt about it, but now it is our turn to have the faith for the two of you."

"Well …, there you go," said Marty. "The Queen Mother has spoken her decree. Now as much as I would like to visit with you, I think you should get Joan back here with the kids. Daniel, you and Greg will come with us now and we will drive around the block so the boys won't know you are next door."

"One last thing," Marty interrupted. "I know a guy that can get you some fake IDs." The rest of the family looked at him, this time with surprise. "What are you all looking at? He is a friend and one of my customers!" he said, returning their stares. "Before you leave, let Ted take a photo of you with his thingamajig on his phone," and looking at the three of them, "I will get Avrohom to make them today and find a way to get them to you. Oh, I know how we can do it. Jill, I will meet you on the Parkway at the rest stop near the Atlantic City Expressway on Monday. How about 9:30 a.m.?"

"You got a date," Jill said, shaking her head, still disturbed that her dad had a way to get some fake IDs, but thankful at the same time. "You might not need them, but I think he's right. You will have them just in case."

"I can't tell you all how much I appreciate your help," Greg said with a deep expression of sincerity.

"Don't thank us, Greg. Thank the Lord who is clearly watching over the two of you."

"Okay," he said, uncharacteristically shy, "I really would, but I don't know how to pray. I have never done it before. Would you do it?" He was asking Jill.

"Sure … Daniel, why are you sitting there with that strange look on your face? Let's pray now," she said, grabbing both of her brother's hands.

Jo got up and took the seat next to Greg, taking his hand in hers and bowing her head, while Ted moved to join them. He knelt in front of him, offering his other hand while Marty just sat across from them watching his family. While everyone was praying, he sat there thanking God for every one of them and placing his son and Greg in The Creator's secure hands.

# Chapter 16

Daniel and Greg were lying uncomfortably under the truck bed cover when Jill and the boys opened the garage door. His dad had dropped them off and Jill had provided them with enough food and water to last for the rest of the weekend. They remained in the basement the entire time, not wanting any of the neighbors to become suspicious if they saw movement in the house. She also supplied them with the kids' sleeping bags, complete with blow-up pillows. Greg was able to rummage around until he found an old TV able to pull in two channels among the clutter.

They discussed what should be on the information sent to the franchise owners and decided the precise moment when it should be emailed. Their plan would depend completely on Sloan agreeing to it. They knew they would be asking a lot of him, especially when they would only be providing circumstantial information, as Daniel was not willing to divulge the tapes Mari Lee had acquired secretly for him … not yet at least.

There was just no way to gauge the reaction of the owners once they received it. If they figured wrong, it could backfire and, in essence, they would be doing exactly what they believed the senior staff was trying to do and cause more confusion and disharmony. They worked laboriously to make sure they wrote the letter as mere speculation without any accusations. That way they would be legally protected and it was only conjecture. The wording was important, but both of their positions required working closely with POP's legal department and they knew enough to make sure it was presented carefully. But the bottom line was that there would be no way to tell what would happen once POP's rumor mill got hold of it and the owners reacted. Troy agreed to give his uncle and Greg a brand-new box of pencils along with a funny nose pencil sharpener built in. He insisted on sharpening several pencils for him by sticking it up one of the nostrils and twisting it with the enjoyment only a ten-year-old could make while doing it. He made clear that he was only giving it to him on the condition that Uncle Danny would promise to take them to a water park when they visited him in Florida. He was right next door to the kids and not being able to be playing with them was hard, but it had to be that way. He knew, when the time came, he would be the one enjoying the water park more than they would, knowing ahead of time they would be dunking him mercilessly in the pool.

They could hear the boys running ahead of Jill and her calling to them to slow down. The doors of the Ford truck opened as they noisily jumped in. They listened to the exchange between the boys and their mother on the way to school. Daniel was proud of the good mom his sister had turned out to be. Separating from Hal had been hard on her. She was all alone once again when she had accepted the teaching position and moved to Cape May, about an hour from her parents, Ted, and his family. But as tough as it was on her, she always made sure the kids came first. He hoped they would never forget it and understood more clearly now some of the difficulties and sacrifices a single mom has to make.

Once they arrived at the school, she pulled her truck around back to the delivery area next to Frances's Ford Transit. She unhooked the latch of the bed cover before walking with the boys into the school. By the time she returned, they were waiting inside Frances's car.

"Okay, you guys," she said as she hopped in the driver's seat. "I stopped by the office and gave the principal a fast and highly edited version of your story, basically letting her know that you were facing a dangerous situation and needed prayer. She is quite something actually and right now is making an announcement asking the teachers to lead their classes in prayer for you two. Let's see, that's about four hundred kids praying …

so the word is out!" She started the car. "Angels of protection are gathering … AS WE SPEAK," she added, confidently smiling.

"Wow, that's amazing," Greg said.

"Yes, it is amazing," Jill said, then explaining, "Greg, for someone who has a deep and close relationship with God, faith is a tangible substance … a substance," she repeated, "something real and solid that God gives us when we need help. It is available just for the asking to sincere believers. The Bible says in Hebrews that faith is the *substance* of things hoped for and the evidence of things not seen.[22] God answers all sincere prayers made to Him in faith. When children pray, they do it with a childlike faith. You ought to hear my kids."

"Boy, the apple didn't fall far from the tree with you two," Greg said, poking fun at the two of them. "You sound just like your brother, Jill."

"She's just louder," Daniel teased, prompting her to remove one hand from the wheel and give him a swat. "You do know you are on my short list right now, so I wouldn't press it if I were you. Don't forget, you owe me."

"She's right though, Greg. One time I needed an answer to prayer so badly that I drove all the way to her house from Pennsylvania …"

"Your sister's prayers are that strong?" he interrupted.

"No, it wasn't hers I wanted. Clay is the one with the most faith in that family. After I got there, I made her wake him up so that he could pray with me."

"Yeah, I remember that time," she said, reflecting.

"I really do think Clay is a special child. Troy is too, Jill. I didn't mean it that way, but Clay prays in a way that you can tell he is communicating directly with God."

"So did you get the answer to your prayer?"

"Funny, but I don't remember what I was praying for," Daniel said, "only that Clay was praying. Greg, prayer grows into such a way of life that it is like breathing. You do it naturally all day long from incident to

---

[22] **Hebrews 11:1** Now faith is the substance of things hoped for, the evidence of things not seen.

incident and there are so many answers that it is impossible to remember all of them."

Jill took the exit into the Garden State Parkway rest area. Seeing her dad, she pulled next to his SUV and they transferred into it. Moments later Ted's car pulled up and he joined them.

"The three girls are at school, Danny, and they are disappointed they aren't going to see you this trip," Ted said as he slid in next to his sister and Greg.

"Tell them I'll make it up to them," Daniel said, nodding seriously.

"Look, son," Marty began, "here are the fake IDs." He handed the IDs to them. "Your brother went with me and gave him the photos from his phone."

Daniel looked at his ID and scoffed. "Really? Ted, this is not funny," he said angrily.

"Why, what's the matter with it?" Marty asked, concerned.

"My smart-aleck brother is the matter," he said, irritated and looking at Ted. "Now is not the time for games."

Jill grabbed the fake Alabama license and laughed.

"What does it say?" asked Greg.

She read it aloud slowly. "Robert Banks." She smirked. "Rob Banks, get it?"

Everyone in the car tried unsuccessfully to suppress their laughter, including Daniel.

"What does mine say?" Jill looked at Greg's.

"Yours is okay …, Harry Jones."

"Danny, you know if I can put that name on such an important piece of identification that I believe, without a doubt, that you're going to be okay. I only wish I could go along with you two," he said sadly, bending his head down and reaching into his pocket then quickly pulling another one out. "Oh look!" he said, feigning surprise. "Another fake ID. What do you know about that!"

Daniel would have tried to tell him that he would be in too much danger and he had three kids and a wife to take care of, but he knew it would be a total waste of time. It was one thing to have his sister drop them off. She would be safe, but knowing his brother, it would be a different thing. At that moment, he realized that it is one thing to have faith for yourself, but quite another for the people you love. *Now was when the rubber would meet the road where his faith was concerned,* he thought to himself.

"Thank God for family," he said, giving him a warm smile while raising his hand and moving it toward the side of his face touching it affectionately, then quickly moving his hand to the top of his head and mussing his hair vigorously.

"Stop it!" he said, pulling away sharply while stroking his hair back into place. The family laughed again knowing how much he hated anyone touching his perfectly groomed hair, and because of that, it was often Danny's target. "Forget them killing you. I'm going to do it myself," he said, thrusting his own hand at the loose skin of Daniel's inner thigh, pinching and holding it, causing Daniel to scream out in pain.

"Okay, okay, let me go. I'm sorry…"

At that Jill burst into tears. "No," she said, getting hold of herself and wiping her eyes with the back of her wrist. "It's just that," she hesitated, "I don't think Ted is supposed to go. I don't know why and I know I would want him there too if it were me …"

"I agree with your sister," Marty interrupted. "Danny, the Lord has protected you this far and in miraculous ways. My sense is that He will continue what He began and that you need to go through this without your brother. This is your trial of faith."[23] Then he turned his attention to Greg. "Son, the Lord used you to uncover all this. Had it not been for you, Danny would not have been able to put two and two together. My sense is that God's hand is upon both of you, not just Daniel. This trial of faith is for the two of you."

"Hear, hear," said Jill, grabbing Ted's hand. "No one in this car doubts

---

[23] **1 Peter 1:7** That the trial of your faith, being much more precious than of gold that perisheth, though it be tried with fire, might be found unto praise and honor and glory at the appearing of Jesus Christ.

you would be there for your brother. Up until now, Danny's entire focus has been on the Lord protecting him. If you go along, you know he will be looking to you … like we both did growing up."

Ted knew he was hearing wisdom, but still didn't like the idea of letting him go without his help. "What's Danny going to do if…"

"Theo," Marty interrupted, "I'm your dad and I know how much you love your brother, but this is your test of faith as well. I believe the Lord wants us all to trust Him and only Him. No matter the outcome and no matter how hard it is, we need to put these two in the Lord's hands. Now we must trust in that and pray." Turning to face forward, he started the car. "It is time we all get on with the day."

Daniel got out of the SUV along with Ted. He grabbed his arm before he got into his car and pulled him in to a big hug. "I love you, big brother."

"Go on, get out of here," Ted said, pushing him back a bit not liking emotional moments. When he got into his Corvette, he rolled down his window. "Stay safe," he said soberly. "I'll be praying for you, little brother." He put the car in gear and, as he started to move away, yelled out his window. "I still think God could've used my help. And if you meet a bad guy, don't just talk him to death!"

Daniel walked up to his dad's window, reaching in to hold his hand for a moment. Nothing was spoken but much was communicated.

"Okay, you two, I want you both to take care of each other, and Greg, come back to visit us," Marty said. "Be off with you now. Vaya con Dios." Daniel smiled. This was the last thing his dad would say before he left. It meant, go with God.

The trip to Paramus was uneventful, but it did give him a chance to talk with his sister about her separation. "I had a call from Hal about a month ago and wanted to wait until we were together before I mentioned it."

"What did he say?" Jill asked with interest.

"He wanted to know how you and the kids were doing."

"Why didn't he call me. I am not angry with him?"

"Who knows, but he did say something I thought I should pass along.

He thinks you took the kids and moved across country because he was a bad father."

"Really? I don't know why he would think that. That's not the reason. It was the only place I could go that would be good for the kids. There were other reasons that I don't want to talk with you about."

"And I won't ask. But I thought I should tell you, that's all. I don't know what happened between you two, but I do think he still loves you. You do know that not every separation has to end in divorce. Enough said."

When they reached Paramus, Jill drove the van into the shopping center and pulled to a stop in front of POP's Office Supply. They said their goodbyes and watched her leave.

Unbeknown to them, at just about the same time, someone was calling Jill's school asking to speak with her. The receptionist informed them that she was off for the day, but when they mentioned they were old friends of hers, further explained she had taken a personal day because her brother was in town.

# CHAPTER 17

Daniel and Greg walked into the busy store and immediately saw Sloan talking with one of his managers. When he noticed them, they were greeted with a big smile as he started heading toward them. "Hey … as I live and breathe, two corporate bigwigs instead of one. To what do I owe this pleasure?"

They greeted him, shaking hands. "If you have a few minutes, we would like to discuss something with you in your capacity as the president of the POP's Franchise Owners Association."

"Sure, let's go into my office," he said, gesturing them toward his office and addressing his manager while he was walking, letting her know he did not want to be disturbed. Sloan sat down behind his messy desk, shuffling papers around, and asked them to take a seat. "What's going on?"

Sloan listened intensely without interrupting as he wanted to let them get it all out before he responded. They filled Sloan in on the details; however, they left out the attempts made on their lives as they were afraid that kind of information getting loose could cause its own catastrophe, should it ever make its way to the rumor mill. They kept it strictly to the business aspects and the unknown effects it could have on the franchise owners. Finally, he was ready to respond.

"Well," he said, "that is quite a story. If I heard it from anyone else, I would think it was sour grapes, but coming from you two, I am persuaded to take it a step further. I am not willing to send anything out to the owners … yet." He picked up the news release that they had given him and looked it over.

"What do you mean when you say a step further?" Greg asked.

"What you are saying involves the stock market and my brother is a trader on Wall Street. I'd like to get him on the phone and see if he even thinks what you are suggesting is possible."

"We'd like that, too," Greg offered, confirming it with a nod from Daniel.

Sloan speed-dialed Darryl, put him on speaker, and placed the phone in the center of his desk so they all could hear.

"Sloan, what's up, buddy—I'm kind of busy now—is it important?" he said in one long and fast sentence.

"Actually, this time it is."

"Hold on." All three could hear him begin shouting orders to others in his office and finally the words, "and close the door on your way out … and don't slam—"All three heard the slamming of a door.

"Okay, Sloan, you have my attention," Darryl said.

"I have two men with me that work for the corporate office of my franchise. They have come to me with quite a story. Daniel is the marketing manager and Greg from the sales department." All exchanged hellos. "I told them if anyone else told me this story, I would have dismissed it and thought them delusional. But I do trust these two and they are both well respected by other owners."

"Okay, got the picture. So what's up?"

"In a nutshell, the franchise was recently taken over by a company trading on the stock market. The old regime has been replaced by a new team of officers, who now report to the new company."

"Nothing unusual there. In fact, that is quite normal and I bet the franchise owners don't like it."

"Right, but at the last Conclave, four of the owners had suspicions of their own and met with these guys. They were concerned because they were hearing stories that the new team was making special deals with owners that go against the franchise's historical policies. You know, issues that can become incendiary, especially in a franchise situation when everyone has a vested interest in its success and not just in the stock prices. Additionally, this new team turned down solid marketing opportunities that could have proven to be significantly beneficial to POP's owners, according to Greg and Daniel. Lastly, when they checked the stock prospectus, they found the president and several of the vice presidents came from companies that filed Chapter Eleven bankruptcy. Are you with me so far?"

"I'm listening."

"Daniel and Greg suspect that the new company is purposely working to send them into bankruptcy. Now this could be a coincidence, but three of the owners who were in the meeting at Conclave died while returning home, and although they have not said it, by the way they look and sound, I think they are afraid for their lives." Sloan nodded to them. "It could all be a coincidence, as there were several thousand people attending who were traveling home, but it is unusual, and I thought I would get your take on it as it relates to the market."

They could hear Darryl repositioning himself in his chair as it squeaked. "Well, I have heard some stories of something like they are describing, but I do not know if there is any truth to it or not." He paused. "What is the name of the company that took them over?"

Daniel answered. "Balaam Basor Investments out of Chicago."

"Whoa! Now you've gone and said it." They listened to his chair squeak again. "Sloan, I think you may have a problem if they are the ones that bought your franchise. I have not heard one good word about them, and in fact, if you were to tell me you wanted to invest in them, I would advise you not to do it. I think they may even have some underworld connections. Not a good company to be involved with in any way."

Sloan watched as fear crossed the faces of Greg and Daniel. "Then you think these guys might be right?"

"Could be! If they are, I think all of you might be in for a world of hurt. I mentioned I have heard rumors. Let me tell you the scenario and you tell me if it is a match. New company comes into an enterprise that is well positioned in the market and their stocks are trading at a high price. The key is that the next company would be an up and comer with stocks trading at a drastically lower price. The top company is mismanaged and within a short amount of time, the company collapses and the stocks go up on the lesser company, or companies, and their smaller investments go through the roof."

"That's it," said Greg, "but why would they do that? They would lose the money they invested to take over the top company. Wouldn't they lose millions?"

"Well, yes and no," Darryl said. "It depends on a lot of factors. Let's say that in the industry we are talking about, there are several other companies competing for, in this case, POP's Office Supply stock purchases. If a company like Balaam Basor, which has a thousand sub-companies that are hard to track, made heavy stock investments … indirectly …" he stressed and paused for a few moments, letting them catch up to the concept, "so the investments were cloaked and through companies that in turn owned other companies and investments and then through another layer of companies they owned and so on and on … the result being that the lower-priced stocks could increase their value overnight, in theory at least, *if*— and that is a big *if*—the top company's stocks suddenly fall for some reason. If that were to happen, a lot of money could be made as the stocks in the lesser companies begin to soar as investors dump POP's stock and make purchases in the lower-cost stock which now looks certain to increase in value."

"That's amazing," Sloan said at a loss for words.

"Not only that, Sloan, but with so many sub-companies and shadow companies, they could also be making *calls* and *puts*. To make it simple, investors buy calls when they think the share price of the underlying security will rise, or sell a call if they think it will fall. Put options give the holder the right to sell an underlying asset at a specified price. In other words, there are many ways money could be made in addition to the rise and fall of the stock price itself."

"So we were right about it the whole time," Greg said.

"Hold on," Darryl said. "There's more. Once everything falls apart, instead of filing Chapter Seven bankruptcy, they file for Chapter Eleven."

"What's the difference?" asked Daniel.

"The main difference between Chapter Seven and Chapter Eleven bankruptcy is that under a Chapter Seven bankruptcy filing, the debtor's assets are sold off to pay the lenders, the creditors; whereas in Chapter Eleven, the debtor negotiates with creditors to alter the terms of the loan without having to liquidate, or sell off, asset."

"Are you telling me that they can reorganize the franchise by negotiating with creditors to lower the amount they pay to them?" Sloan asked.

"Not only that, Sloan, but since you are a franchise, my money would be on them wanting to increase their franchise fees temporarily to allow them to get themselves back on track. Think about it, the franchise owners would have a lot to lose if they didn't do it."

"Exactly. But I think there could be more. In this case, I think they would take all the advantages that Chapter Eleven gives them, then bring in another team who specializes in reorganization, then build the business the right way; the sales increase, the franchise owners are happy again, the stock eventually goes up and they all make money."

"What a bunch of snakes!" Daniel said vehemently. "A few win and almost everyone else loses."

"And I hate to tell you this, Daniel, but that's when you might even see them adding the program you presented to them that they turned down. If it was a good one, you can bet they will do their best to resurrect the idea. Listen, you guys, I'd love to stay and chat, but I got a lot of chaos going on here and I gotta get back to work. Sloan, catch you later, buddy."

The phone disconnected.

The three of them sat quietly for a few moments, none of them knowing what exactly to say. In different ways to each of them, the conversation with Darryl had blown their worlds to bits.

Finally, Sloan picked up the letter he earlier had pretty much dismissed and started reading it out loud.

*****

Dear POP's Franchise Owner,

While we were at the Conclave in Atlantic City, a confidential meeting was held with several franchise owners to discuss their concerns with the new senior staff. That meeting included Dottie Daye, Lance Schiffold, Jerry Jones, and Sam Salerno, of whom many of you know. In addition, they had asked both Greg Martinez and myself to attend.

Although we had information at the time we could have shared with them, we did not, being concerned that it could be divisive and inflammatory. Rather, we decided to inform the President of the Franchise Owners Association, then he and the officers would decide how to handle these speculations. We have written this memo and given it to Sloan Dickenson to be used as he and the officers see fit. Rather than tell you what that information is, we suggest each of you read closely this year's *POP's Office Supply Prospectus,* which was either sent out recently or you should be receiving shortly, unless there was a problem with its mailing.

From my own standpoint, I first became concerned when the senior staff was not interested in a pilot program presented by the marketing department that was arranging, along with officials of the United States Post Office, for a test program which would install a self-service drop box to be placed in each of the office supply locations as a convenience for both their customers and ours. We believe it would have been an advantageous program for both parties and would have been implemented at no cost to you. We do not know why they made that decision, but we think it is information that should be shared with you.

By the time you read this, both Greg and I will have submitted our resignation as neither of us believe we can transfer the loyalty we shared for Will and Winnie, and to all of you owners, to the new team. We will miss all of you and certainly wish you the best.

We both add that all the information we have just shared with you are merely concerns and is not intended to demean the reputation or integrity of the senior staff, who, we have been told by some of our franchise owners, are doing a good job.

_____

**Daniel Davidson**
**Marketing**

_____

**Greg Martinez**
**Senior Sales Manager**

*****

"I will talk to the other officers and I expect that we will be sending this to the owners, but now we have to figure out what to do with the two of you. Was I correct when I guessed you both were afraid for your lives?" Sloan asked compassionately, realizing what the two men must have been going through.

Daniel started to tear up, clearing his throat and shaking it off, and was able to pull himself together before responding. "They tried to kill me twice. I have never been so scared in my life."

"I managed to avoid them until Daniel brought me into it with the FBI?" said Greg.

"The FBI? You didn't mention that," Sloan said.

They explained they thought it would have been just too much to believe that they thought the FBI was somehow involved, but Sloan was not at all surprised.

"If the company is that big and nefarious, they are going to have all their people in the right places," he said. "Now let's figure out what your next step is and how to keep you guys safe."

# Chapter 18

**666**

Lucifer paced back and forth, his fury welling up from deep within. Daniel, and now Greg along with him, had evaded his death traps, not once, but several times now. His pride was burning to his core that his former controller was still maintaining sovereignty in the situation. All because of this newly increased and disgusting faith Daniel was practicing. *We shall see about that.* So far, it had consistently cut off his evil at every phase he and Havoc had implemented, seriously frustrating each and every one of their snares.

"You low-living slithering idiot," he said, addressing Havoc. "I send you out to do a man's job and you return beaten by a mere human. You are now vermin to me. May you rot where you stand and be ashamed before all your subordinates."

Lucifer then waved his hand and a picture of his cowering former top demon was displayed before the eyes of all his underlings. Thin leather straps, with pieces of metal hooks imbedded in each of the four-foot multi-tailed whips, began to flagellate the demon who had lost favor.

"Let this be a lesson to all of you to NEVER fail when I send you on an undertaking. You return successful from your assignment or you do not return at all."

"Ruination and Furor come forth," he commanded. "Remove this vile parasite and then return to me. I shall send both of you this time. They think Sloan is a friend and perhaps he is, but we own the friends he will be calling upon to assist these two. What they intend to do in secret, we shall exploit and death shall reign before they enter again into the glorious state of California."

Satan laughed loudly and deeply at all he had accomplished in the once highly desirable state; and then he laughed even louder, sending reverberating shivers through each and every one of his cruel spirits … the trembling racing through them all the way down to their forked tails.

777

Haszik sat on a boulder in the midst of the stream, enjoying the sounds and sights of nature that surrounded him. His arrows, now in a nearly empty quiver slung over his shoulder, supernaturally replenished itself with the appropriate size for the bow that rested on the rock next to him. He was lying back on his elbows with his eyes closed enjoying the warmth of the Son shining down on him. He was surrounded by huge weeping willow trees whose roots were strong like himself, as they had grown next to the river.[24] To all angels, the willow tree represented strength, stability, and standing firm while bearing up against the greatest of challenges.

Melchior, who was resting on one of its upper branches, floated down to join him, stopping just high enough over the water to allow his foot to dangle into its coolness. "Our Creator has blessed us with a time of rejuvenation and I expect our assignment shall continue soon. Have you been observing your friend Daniel?"

"Of course, he has not been out of my sight for one minute. Old Slewfoot has not been resting and neither have I." Haszik dipped his fingers into the water, letting it wash over his hand. "You know, Melchior, I really love my charge. His faith has grown so much in the past few days and I am so proud of him. Proud of what God has done with him, you understand?"

"Yes, and it is as it should be, Haszik," his mentor continued. "God allows us to have an attachment to our humans on purpose as he wants us to think of them as brothers … family. You do know that humans, as a creation, were formed to be just a little lower than us, don't you?"[25]

"I do know that, but I don't really understand what it means."

"Haszik, it means that when they achieve a closeness to our Lord Jesus Christ, they will begin moving with the spirit of God. Those who truly know Him, not just in word, but in deed, will do even greater works

---

[24] **Psalm 1:3** And he shall be like a tree planted by the rivers of water, that bringeth forth his fruit in his season; his leaf also shall not wither; and whatsoever he doeth shall prosper.

[25] **Hebrews 2:6–8** But one in a certain place testified, saying, What is man, that thou art mindful of him? or the son of man, that thou visitest him? Thou madest him a little lower than the angels; thou crownedst him with glory and honor, and didst set him over the works of thy hands: Thou hast put all things in subjection under his feet. For in that he put all in subjection under him, he left nothing that is not put under him. But now we see not yet all things put under him.

than He did while he lived in the flesh on this earth.[26] But sadly, many attending God's church remain in sin and operate only in the false gifting of the great counterfeiter, and without knowing it, remain as their father the devil would have it."[27]

"Will Greg be like that?"

"We do not know. We can only watch and assist him. He will be given the opportunity the same as everyone who comes to the Lord." He hesitated. "It is clear to us at the moment that he has been called by the Lord for this task, but we are not given the knowledge if he will eventually be chosen. Only the Lord can decide that."[28]

"Who are the ones that are chosen then?" asked Haszik.

"Only those who sincerely respond to the call. Those who repent from their sinful ways and deeply receive Christ in faith and in a visibly life-changing way. Jesus calls them the chosen." Melchior removed his foot from the cool water. "Haszik, I think our charges will be needing us soon. We must depart now as our time of rest is complete." Melchior took in a deep breath and expelled it in a wisp of air within a gentle breeze that made the leaves of the drooping willows begin to sway. Swiftly and without notice, all that was left was the beauty and sound of trickling water flowing around the rocks with birds chirping in song, briskly flapping their wings … singing in their own way praises to their mighty God and thanking Him for their daily sustenance.[29]

*****

---

[26] **John 14:12** Verily, verily, I say unto you, He that believeth on me, the works that I do shall he do also; and greater works than these shall he do; because I go unto my Father.

[27] **John 8:44** Ye are of your father the devil, and the lusts of your father ye will do. He was a murderer from the beginning, and abode not in the truth, because there is no truth in him. When he speaketh a lie, he speaketh of his own: for he is a liar, and the father of it.

[28] **Matthew 22:14** For many are called, but few are chosen.

[29] **Matthew 6:26** Behold the fowls of the air: for they sow not, neither do they reap, nor gather into barns; yet your heavenly Father feedeth them. Are ye not much better than they?

"Actually, I have an idea about the safest thing we can do right now," Daniel said, addressing Sloan. "We have been told enough times there is nothing we can do to help from here on out anyway, but we would like to live through this, and I think the safest thing for us to do is to go back to corporate headquarters and stand up to them face to face in front of all the employees."

"Really," Sloan said, surprised and with a tinge of admiration. "Why would you do that?"

"We have our reasons," Daniel said. "Just know that we have done all we can do to help you at this point and now we have to work to save ourselves. The problem is how do we get to Calabasas. I am not really ready to face another flight at the moment; plus, I think that would be the first place they would look. When we left Washington, D.C., the FBI thought we were on the way back to my home in Florida, but once we realized we didn't trust the agent, we had to get a little creative."

"Hey, you guys, you're in New Jersey. Everyone in Jersey 'knows people,' if you know what I mean. I'll get right on getting you some fake IDs so you won't have a problem traveling."

"What is with you people?" Greg said, genuinely smiling for the first time in days. "We already have them. Daniel's dad took care of it."

"Welcome to New Jersey, Greg," Sloan said, "and good for your dad, Daniel. It saves me the trouble and this way we can get you moving faster. I have an idea," he said, looking over at a folded wheelchair in his office.

"Let's hear it." Both of them said it at the same time and moved closer to the edge of their seats.

"My mother is in a wheelchair," he nodded toward one sitting against the wall, "and my dad takes her all over the place in it. About a year ago, they took an Amtrak train to Tucson to visit my sister and stayed in a handicapped-accessible room."

"You want one of us to be in a wheelchair … won't that slow us down?"

"Wait, I'm not finished. I was really quite impressed with the accommodation. It is on the bottom level of a two-story train with easy exits at the stations. Also, it is the only available room that stretches from one side to the other allowing you to see what is going on outside. Plus the windows are one way so you can see out and no one can see in during the daylight hours. At night you just have to keep the curtains closed. It also has its own bathroom and meals are brought directly to your room, so once you are on board, you will never have to leave or be seen by anyone until you get to LA."

"That does sound good," Daniel said, looking at Greg with a smile. "I got dibs on riding in the chair."

"No problem. In fact, I kinda like the idea. That way I get to push you around for a while!"

"In your dreams," Daniel said sarcastically.

"Shoot," Sloan said, closing his eyes for a second with a frustrated look on his face. "I just thought of a problem. If you take the train you will have a regular coach seat from Manhattan to Pittsburgh. But then the rooms are accessible the rest of the way to LA. The other options would be the bus or renting a car."

"The bus would have too many stops and I just don't like that idea. But I do like the idea of being surrounded by people," Daniel said.

"Maybe if we dress in disguises we could get away with it. I think it would be more secure than traveling on a bus," Greg said. "And a car? No way, not such a good idea, too isolated. If they were able to track us, there is a lot of empty interstate between the mid-west and LA ... I've driven it before." He held up his fingers in the shape of the gun and moved his thumb forward as he said the word *bang*.

"Then the train it shall be," Sloan said. "I have a Santa outfit with a contoured pillow in front to make it look natural. One of you can wear it under your clothes. It will make you look fatter and you can dye your hair to change your appearance." He paused, thinking. "I will use my connections anyway to make sure you get the best seats closest to the exits and on the first level. I'll give them a call."

"Sure," Daniel said. "Thanks."

"I haven't shaved since I was in Lake Arrowhead and it is already starting to grow in," Greg said, rubbing his face. "I can just leave it like it is, add a few gray highlights to my hair, and wear a Mexican sombrero. I will fit right in traveling through the southwest. What do you think, guys?"

"You will look like a real Mexican hombre," Daniel said, rolling his eyes in fun.

"Make fun if you want to, but I spoke Spanish before I learned to speak English. It might even come in handy."

"Point taken," Daniel said, patting his friend on the back. "You know, seriously, I am glad to have you along to go through all this."

"Yeah, I know … we're brothers from another mother," Greg said. "Are we supposed to hug now, half-wit?"

"Not unless you want to be the one in the wheelchair," Daniel shot back in fun.

A few minutes later, Sloan had taken care of the reservations. "Here's what we got, guys," he said, laying a note on his desk with times and dates. "Since there are no handicapped rooms until you get to Pittsburgh, I booked you two wheelchair seats on the first level, one of you in the wheelchair and the other next to you. There are fewer people on that level and harder to get to, so I am hoping it will be safer. From Pittsburgh to Chicago you will have an accessible room on the first level. Then in Chicago you transfer to one of Amtrak's super-liners and will have another accessible room the rest of the way to Los Angeles. I expect you would be pretty safe from then on."

"So, all we have to do is make it to Chicago before we feel safe," Greg said sarcastically.

"Sorry, guys, but it was the best I could do. The handicapped rooms were booked and I was only able to get the one from Chicago through the connections I told you about. I wish there was a different way, but this is the only thing I could come up with," Sloan said. "Oh, and here." Sloan handed them two phones. "I had my manager run down to Best Buy, a few doors away, and pick up some burner phones. If you have a problem, call me. I have one for myself and will keep it nearby just in case there is an emergency. Right now I don't think we can be too careful."

Greg smiled and didn't bother telling him they already had extra phones just in case they needed them. "We really appreciate it."

The three made plans as to when to send out the email, assuming that the rest of the board agreed to it, and spent the remainder of the time getting ready for the trip.

# CHAPTER 19

Sloan borrowed his parents' handicapped van and dropped Daniel and
Greg off in front of the Amtrak station in Manhattan. They rehearsed
their new personas on the way to the terminal and had Sloan laughing
so hard that he had tears in his eyes while he was driving. He had to beg
them to stop before they got into an accident. By the time they got out of
the van and into the terminal, they had their roles down pat.

Pennsylvania Station is the busiest commuter hub in the western
hemisphere, and when they arrived, it seemed most of them had shown
up all at once. They were immediately thrust into the midst of people
who were whizzing by one another like players in some kind of a dodge
ball video game, occasionally bumping into one another but most able
to maneuver through the masses unscathed in typical New York fashion.

Daniel sat leaning forward in his wheelchair as they moved through
the thick pedestrian traffic crisscrossing in front of them. With both arms
waving haphazardly, he grumbled at people in an aggressive New York
voice, demanding they move aside while periodically swatting someone's
travel bag or briefcase, pushing it out of the way. Some would turn and
make an unpleasant comment to the grumpy old man in the wheelchair,
but most just turned to give him a dirty look and kept going.

Greg was getting into his role as a charming Mexican hombre, complete with poncho, leather hat and cowboy boots. He would have looked
quite handsome had it not been for his fake beer belly and the fact he

appeared a little dirty and disheveled. From time to time, as he pushed Daniel to the ticket window, he would make a clicking sound with his mouth and nod in approval as he passed a pretty woman. "Ah, chiquita … very nice … bonita!" he would say, tipping his hat respectfully while keeping the wheelchair steady with the other hand.

The train attendant assisted in helping them position the wheelchair in the space provided, with a seat next to it for Greg. They settled in with a glass of wine and were surprisingly relaxed. The first few hours before sunset took them through breathtaking views of the green, rolling hills of central Pennsylvania. They were both quiet and mesmerized, looking out the panoramic windows and enjoying a welcome pause in their frightening journey. As it became darker, Daniel decided to take the time with Greg to prepare him for the faith that might be required from both of them.

"Greg, I know you are new to having faith and I'd like to show you a verse from the Bible that I think might help you get through this. Do you mind?" he asked.

"A few weeks ago I would have told you to go fly a kite, but now, after the things I have experienced, I would have to say yes, and thanks. I would appreciate it."

Daniel took out his prepaid smartphone, pulled up the Bible app he downloaded earlier, located 1 Peter 1:7 and read it aloud. "*That the trial of your faith, being much more precious than of gold that perisheth, though it be tried with fire, might be found unto praise and honour and glory at the appearing of Jesus Christ.*" He put the phone back down on his lap and continued. "When this started, God all of a sudden became very real to me and not just a person in the Bible. To me this has been the scariest time of my life. If anyone can understand what I am saying, I think you can."

"Yes, I will agree to that," Greg said, taking in a gulp of air and expelling it slowly through pursed lips. "I don't think I could ever describe to anyone the sense of helplessness I was going through when I was in Lake Arrowhead. Now, as scary as it still is, it is somehow different … livable … even hopeful."

"Yes, you got it. It is different, because now you know that you are not going through it alone … and I don't mean with me. I mean that somehow the spiritual realm has become more visible, for lack of another word."

"I know what you mean."

"At some point, I started thinking of this verse and what it really means in the middle of a crisis. It says the trial of our faith is *precious*. That word really stuck out to me. I mean, I can see that faith is valuable because if you really have it, fear disappears. But here we are with hit men trying to kill us and somehow the Bible tells us this is a precious time of our lives? I mean, give me a break! I am a believer and I find it hard to understand."

Greg thought about it before responding. "Precious means something valued greatly. Right now I don't see that is possible at all … but …" He paused again.

"But what?" Daniel asked, searching for the answer himself.

"Well, after we get through this, and I am beginning to think that we might, it will be an experience that I can never erase from my life. I guess I can see that once you have any kind of faith, it can be built up. If we do value it and really know, without any doubt, that God is on our side, then it really does become precious. Doesn't it?"

"Exactly, I couldn't have said it better myself. And there is another thing I have learned, but I do not know if I can put it into words." He paused, trying to find the right way to explain it. "It's like the bad experiences are separated by times that have allowed me to rest. Like when I went to Rome. It was awful, then I spent time with Elisabetta and Toni. Then after my trip back I had you and then my family. Then Sloan and now just being able to look out the window at this beauty and feeling relaxed even for a moment, is like feeling God's love in the midst of the most nerve-wracking time of our lives."

Greg groaned quite thoughtfully as he considered Daniel's words. "Do you think David in the Bible felt that way when he went into battle? I mean, do you think he ever got past the fear?"

"It's funny you say that, because I have been thinking of him, too. I bet that after a few wars he began to have confidence that everything would turn out well. I mean, it sounds like he had a lot of hand-to-hand combat with swords and shields on the battlefield with thousands of others dying around him, but he lived to a very old age. And yet, throughout his life the one personality trait you see over and over is his faith."

"What do you mean? I don't understand." Greg seemed puzzled.

"Let's see …," Daniel said, trying to think of way he could answer. "Do you know the story of David and Goliath?"

"Sure, as a kid. David fought against a giant."

"Yes, but before he stood up to the giant, his faith had already been tested through other kinds of trials."

"How's that?"

"Well, as a shepherd boy, while he was tending his father's sheep, he fought with both a lion and a bear so that by the time he confronted Goliath, his experience had increased to a point where he was confident the Lord would protect him.[30] He was ready for Goliath by the time he met him, get it? God had already prepared him. And the Lord did that for his entire life. You can read the story in 1 Samuel 7 if you would like to."

"Yea, I'd like to."

After the conversation, Greg downloaded the Bible app on his phone and read about David until it was time for them to change trains in Pittsburgh. Periodically, he would read something about the story out loud.

"Hey, Daniel, this is interesting. I didn't know he killed a good guy! Wow, he committed adultery, had a baby from it, then stole the other guy's wife and had him killed. Man, it sounds like a Hollywood movie," Greg said while Daniel laughed.

"And after all that sin, God still refers to David as a man after his own heart."[31]

---

[30] **1 Samuel 17:37** David said moreover, The Lord that delivered me out of the paw of the lion, and out of the paw of the bear, he will deliver me out of the hand of this Philistine. And Saul said unto David, Go, and the Lord be with thee.

[31] **Acts 13:22** And when he had removed him, he raised up unto them David to be their king; to whom also he gave testimony, and said, I have found David the son of Jesse, a man after mine own heart, which shall fulfil all my will.

"Get out of here, you can't be serious?" Greg asked, genuinely shocked.

"Yes, I am," Daniel said. "I think there are a lot of things about God and the people He loves that will surprise you."

"All my life I knew about God, but I never took the time to get to know Him. I never understood that it was really possible."

"Now is your chance, my friend," Daniel said, encouraging him as the train slowed in its final approach to the station.

Fortunately, the transfer was short and they were able to board the train to Chicago immediately. The transfer went well. The only thing noticeable was that, at one point, a man glanced at them in what seemed to Greg just a little bit too long of a moment, but when they discussed it, they decided it was probably just his imagination. They got settled again, and soon after it left the station. They fell into an uncomfortable and fitful sleep, but one they sorely needed.

They woke up early and were enjoying their second cup of coffee after breakfast before arriving in Chicago when the waiter came to take away their trays. "Sirs, does your trip end here in Chicago or are you transferring to another train?" he asked while removing their trays.

"Transferring. We are catching the Southwest Chief and have a handicapped room on that one. How long is the layover?" Daniel asked.

"That would be just over six hours. It leaves at three p.m."

Both of them sat up. "What?" said Greg. "I thought it was a short layover."

"No, sir, it always leaves at three p.m."

Daniel quickly pulled out the travel envelope and opened his ticket to confirm the departure time. He looked up at the waiter and then to Greg, letting his hands drop to his lap as he looked at Greg. "He's right ... three p.m. How could Sloan have missed that?"

"Gentlemen, if you are looking for something to do, might I suggest you take the ten-minute walk to Sears Tower," he said. "When you leave the front entrance of the terminal, just look up and you'll see it. Then go down Adams Street, take a right turn on Wacker Drive and you are there. It's not a bad walk if you are pushing a chair." He directed his comment to

Greg. "It is the tallest building in Chicago and the view is outstanding. You will find a number of good restaurants for lunch along the way," he added before taking his leave with the trays and closing the door behind him.

"Daniel, what's the matter with you? Why didn't you look at the schedule?"

"Me? How about you? And it was Sloan who took care of the tickets," he said, severely irritated.

"You are really going to blame him? Next thing you will be telling me that you think he is one of the bad guys, too," Greg said angrily.

"You know you really can be a jerk sometimes."

"Ditto!" Greg said, calming himself down. "I think the waiter has the best idea. If I am going to be in Chicago, the city our senior staff comes from, I want to be someplace that is very busy and where we can blend in with the tourists."

"Yeah, right. We really do blend in!" he said sarcastically. "Me in a wheelchair being pushed around by Pancho in a sombrero. We will fit right in. We won't stand out at all … bozo!" he said insultingly.

Both of the men sat there looking away from each other, trying to regain their composure. After a minute of tense silence, Daniel was the first one to speak. "I apologize, Greg. That was out of line."

"Me, too, Daniel. I am sorry. I think we both just got scared. I think going to the Sears Tower is a good idea."

"So Sears Tower it is."

"Onward Christian soldiers!" Greg said, trying to bring a little levity into the situation. "Bozo, huh?" he added. "By the way, I really am very sorry for the mean, awful, accurate word I used to describe you."

# CHAPTER 20

Daniel leaned back in his wheelchair and looked straight up the side of the Sears Tower. From his position on the sidewalk, he literally felt the dizzying effect of looking up all one hundred and ten stories of its glass exterior, straight up.

They watched tourists getting on and off sightseeing buses and walking through the revolving doors to visit the tower's world-famous skydeck. For the moment, they felt like two sightseers on vacation. Those visitors would enjoy a high-speed elevator ride that would make some stomachs queasy, and they would look at videos on the way up as they passed the heights of other famous landmarks like the Statue of Liberty, The Eiffel Tower, and the Empire State Building. Once at the top, almost every one of them would take photos while standing on a thick glass floor allowing them to gaze all the way back down to the ground far below.

They would have joined them, but Greg admitted he had acrophobia, a fear of heights. Daniel told him he understood, suggesting instead that they go around the corner to see the lobby of the giant office building to get a look at its business end. He remembered reading that American Airlines had rented out many of the floors of one of the high rises in Chicago and thought it might be interesting to find out if this was the one. Greg pushed him around to the front of the building on Wacker Drive.

As they reached the main entrance, Greg suddenly froze and stood motionless as terror assaulted every one of his senses. All he could do was stand there looking above the entrance, tapping Daniel on the shoulder.

"Yes, this really is impressive, isn't it?" Daniel said, looking through the glass at the beautiful lobby.

"Daniel, look up."

"I know, it is an incredibly tall buildin…" He didn't finish the word as he read the name written above the entrance in huge bold letters. WILLIS TOWERS, 233 SOUTH WACKER DRIVE. He raised his head to look at Greg while an immense rush of disbelief shot through his body, triggering his heart rate to instantly soar, causing spasmodic shortness of breath and a choking sensation that caused him to cough out loud until he was able get it under control.

At that same split second, they both realized they should have known that the famous Sears Tower was renamed the Willis Towers and was the home of Balaam Besor, the company that purchased their franchise. Then, as if it had been somehow orchestrated, their attention was drawn to a cab pulling up to the curb not far from where they were standing. Becoming suddenly frozen, they both watched in panic as Melinda got out of the taxi followed by Greg's new boss, Ray Shaman.

Greg wanted to turn the wheelchair around and run, but his legs were unable to move as he watched in horror and slow motion as Melinda glanced in his direction making eye contact with him for a brief second. Ordering Daniel to turn his face away from them, he forced his will to overtake his actions. He then slowly turned and began pushing the wheelchair in the direction from which they had come. Every one of his fight or flight responses was triggered and screaming for him to break into a run. But he was able to suppress the urge.

They went directly back to the train station, both carrying with them a sense of impending doom, completely freaked out and stressed past any point either of them had been before. Fortunately, the train had arrived early and the attendant allowed them to board right away. Once into their room, Greg locked the door and closed the shades on both sides of the train and sat down at the table, folding his hands and putting his head on top of them.

"How could the two of us forget that the Sears Tower was also known as the Willis Tower? How is that possible, Daniel … and the timing. How is it feasible that we would be standing on the sidewalk at the instant that Melinda and my boss show up? And why in the world would Melinda be with my boss in Chicago in the first place?"

"Greg, I am feeling a little overwhelmed with fear at the moment myself. Would you mind if we prayed together right now? It will help, I promise."

"Of course. But Daniel, I am scared out of my wits. I don't know if it will do any good."

Daniel reached out his hand, placing it on Greg's shoulder. "Yes, it will," he said, closing his eyes and lowering his head. "Dear Jesus, you know exactly what just happened and we are both very scared right now. It is hard for us to not feel that fear, Lord, but we believe you can remove it from us so that we can begin to think straight. We don't have more words right now, so please, in your mercy, please help us. In Jesus name we pray."

"That's it?" Greg asked.

"Yep, that's all we need to do, just consciously put it into His hands with faith backing it up." Daniel looked at Greg. "Any difference?"

"Not a bit, not yet, but maybe I feel like something left me."

"Just trust. It takes a while sometimes, but we have just asked God for His help and He promises that wherever two or more are gathered in His name that He will hear our prayer."[32] Daniel found himself struggling to calm his own fear in order to help his friend. "Greg …, you know how we have been aware of how God has been supernaturally helping us with His perfect timing?"

---

[32] **Matthew 18:19–20** Again I say unto you, That if two of you shall agree on earth as touching any thing that they shall ask, it shall be done for them of my Father which is in heaven. For where two or three are gathered together in my name, there am I in the midst of them.

"Yes, I admit I have been able to see that. Either that or it has been a lot of coincidences."

"Well, the Word says that Satan is like a roaring lion looking for opportunities to slay people who love and serve God.*[33] Melinda and Ray showing up like that and us realizing that the Sears Tower was really the Willis Tower all at the same time is clear evidence of spiritual warfare. But, Greg, the fact that the Lord let us see that gives us an advantage."

"I don't get it. I mean, I see about the timing and everything, but how does it give us an advantage?"

"Because the enemy of our souls, Ole Slew Foot has just shown us his hand and God is the one that allowed us to see. It was meant to strengthen our faith, not to weaken it … not to scare us but to empower us with courage. Get it?"

"Not quite like you do, but I'll work on it," he said in a way that sounded doubtful. "To be honest with you, I don't know if I can take much more of this."

"I know. I feel the same way, Greg." At that instant, the train jerked a few inches forward before tugging ahead a second time, then moving steadily toward Kansas City.

Greg closed the curtains for an instant then jerked it back down.

"Daniel, remember the guy we saw in Pittsburgh that we thought might be looking at us?"

"Yes, why?"

"I just saw him again."

Daniel shot up out the wheelchair and started pacing back and forth in the small area. "Look, let's get hold of Sloan and tell him what is going on. I don't know what he can do, but somebody ought to know." He pulled out his cell phone.

---

[33] **1 Peter 5:8–11** Be sober, be vigilant; because your adversary the devil, as a roaring lion, walketh about, seeking whom he may devour: Whom resist steadfast in the faith, knowing that the same afflictions are accomplished in your brethren that are in the world. But the God of all grace, who hath called us unto his eternal glory by Christ Jesus, after that ye have suffered a while, make you perfect, stablish, strengthen, settle you. To him be glory and dominion for ever and ever. Amen.

"I agree, and you better do it now before we get out of the city and lose cell service."

Sloan had his phone sitting on his desk and immediately answered when it rang. "Hey, how are you? Are you guys okay?" His voice was very concerned.

"Sloan, we got a problem. Did you know we had almost a seven-hour wait between trains in Chicago?"

"It couldn't be helped, it was the only thing available. I didn't tell you because it would've just made you stress longer than you probably did. I am hoping all went well. Did it?"

"No, not exactly." Daniel paused, gathering his thoughts. "To make a long story short, the two of us forgot that Sears Tower is now the Willis Tower and the home of the company that now owns POP's. We freaked when we found that out and then we saw the VP of sales along with the president's secretary getting out of a cab going into the building."

"Man, you guys have bad timing. Did they see you?"

"Greg thinks yes. Melinda glanced our way and it is quite possible she recognized us."

"Where are you now and how far to the next stop?"

"We just left Chicago and arrive in Kansas City about eight hours from now. Why?"

"That means you will be getting there about eleven p.m. local time. Let me see what I can do from this end. I'll get back to you as soon as I can. It is about four p.m. here, so I gotta get off the phone to make some calls. Hang in there you guys. Bye."

The cell phone went dead, leaving them with little more hope than before they made the call.

The porter brought them both dinner on a tray along with a glass of wine and dessert. All the food was picked up uneaten, except for the two glasses of wine. Daniel's burner phone rang. He almost dropped it out of his hand trying to answer it. "Hello, Sloan?"

"Daniel, good news. It appears you have some good friends in the industry."

"Why, what's going on?"

"Do you know Chuck and Sandy Rose?"

"Sure, they own Rose Paper company. They supply most of our stores with copier paper and supplies and are old friends of Will and Winnie."

"Not just Will and Winnie. Evidently of yours as well. When he and his wife were in the area a few months ago, they stopped by and remembered you fondly. He told me he thought you would be the president of POP's someday. Anyway, he has the solution."

"How's that?"

"I hope you don't mind, but I told them what was going on. They have been friends of Will's since before he turned POP's into a franchise and are very loyal to him … and to you, too, so I didn't think you would mind."

"No, of course not."

"He and Sandy are in St. Louis at a meeting. They own a Gulfstream jet and he has agreed to meet you in Kansas City and fly you and Greg the rest of the way to California."

Daniel looked at Greg. "Remember when you said you couldn't take much more? Well, it looks like this nightmare is getting closer to an end, one way or the other. Some friends of Will's and mine own a jet. They are going to pick us up in Kansas City and fly us the rest of the way."

"When you get to Kansas City, just leave the wheelchair and get off the train," Sloan instructed. "Chuck said he was going to hire a limo and meet you, so keep an eye out for him. And Daniel, the email is definitely a go. Give me a call about fifteen minutes before you arrive at headquarters and I will send it out to the owners. I'm sure that will light up their switchboard. If nothing else, it might give you some added protection. They would be stupid to try anything with all that going on and you two being there in front of the employees."

"Okay, but we have another problem. Greg has seen the same guy watching us twice now. Once in Pittsburgh and again just as the train was leaving Chicago. Evidently, Melinda must have passed along the information. They might be waiting for us in Kansas City and Chuck might be in trouble. You better let him know."

"I will. I'll get him back on the phone right away."

"I'm so sorry, Daniel, but I wish I could help you guys when you get there." He paused. "You've been pretty good at getting out of situations so far. I would suggest you keep doing what you've been doing and use that same ingenuity. Keep the faith, Daniel, and tell Greg that we are all pulling for you two. Make it home safe."

They disconnected and Daniel filled Greg in. Wanting to keep himself busy, Greg pulled out a pad of paper and the box of pencils that Troy had given them along with the pencil sharpener that looked like a nose.

"What are you doing?" Daniel asked.

"I'm going to sketch, if you don't mind. It helps me get rid of stress and now is as good a time as any," he said, sticking a pencil up the nostril of the nose-shaped sharpener and twisting it. "That nephew of yours really is a kick." He held the nose up in the air, giving the pencil one more twist and then removing a sharpened pencil. "Let's both try to relax … I can't believe I just said that!"

# CHAPTER 21

Several hours passed and both were lost in their own brooding frame of mind. Daniel watched Greg sketching. "Can I take a look at what you have drawn?"

"Sure," Greg said, handing the pad over to him.

Daniel smiled. "I needed this." He was looking at a picture of an angel with large wings, dressed as a soldier, kneeling on one knee with a sword in one hand and a shield in the other, looking up toward heaven. "Greg, this is really good. I didn't know you were an artist."

"Thanks," he said, spreading the pencils out evenly and running his fingers to and fro over them, making a faint sound on the tabletop. "If we ever needed angels, it would be now. I have drawn this same picture before, but never with the intensity I did this time."

An abrupt knocking on the door interrupted their conversation. "This is the porter. We will be arriving in Kansas City shortly and I would like to turn down your beds for the night."

They looked at each other and nodded, agreeing it was okay to unlock the door.

The door opened and an unfamiliar porter walked into the small room and closed the door behind him. As he turned back facing them, he removed a gun with a silencer from under his white vest. Without hesitation, Greg lunged at the man, knocking him back against the door, causing the gun to fire a hole in the window but missing all three of them.

Daniel went for the man's arms, trying to keep the gun pointed away from them and in doing so lost balance, slamming into Greg. He fell on top of the table, collapsing it into its storage position flat against the wall between the seats, scattering everything that had been on top of it all over the floor.

Daniel continued struggling against the much larger man, who managed to hit him squarely on the head with his elbow, nearly knocking him out cold. As he started falling, his shoulder smashed against the gun, knocking it out of the assassin's hand and onto the floor. It then slid across the room, coming to a stop beside the toilet.

Greg frantically stretched for it, but it was just out of his reach. Simultaneously, Daniel had managed to shake off the pain from the smack to his head and continued pounding the bigger man with his fist, over and over with as much strength as he could.

Greg kept stretching a little bit further, when suddenly he grabbed for a pencil that had fallen to the floor next to him in the melee. Picking up two of the sharpened ones, he jabbed the first deeply into the man's leg while reaching out with the other, trying to jam the point into the silencer so he could pull it closer and get his hand on the gun. The assassin, now fighting for his own life, doubled over in pain as Greg shoved the point into the barrel. Now wounded, the assassin kicked it away from Greg, breaking the pencil with a snap. The gun flew into the wall, bouncing back and landing directly into the hired gunman's hand. With a solid grip on the handle, he stood up waving it at the two of them while catching his breath.

"Move over into this corner," he said, waving the gun and ordering the two of them against the wall. "You two have been causing a lot of grief. Just so you know, this time the bosses called out the big gun to get the job done. That would be me."

Daniel was looking directly at the muzzle of the silencer. "Look, my name is Daniel and this is Greg."

"Shut up, I don't care what your names are."

"Fine, but I think you should know that God has been protecting us and it's your life that is in danger at the moment … not ours."

The big man snarled. "I got to give it to you, you've got guts, but now it's over," he said, pulling the trigger.

Greg and Daniel watched as the gun exploded, blowing a hole into the bottom of the barrel, shattering it into pieces and bending the silencer upward as a blast of fire and then smoke surrounded the gun. The hit man flew backwards, falling then sagging against the wall slowly to the floor. His face and hands were already blackened and bleeding, as the top layers of his skin had been ripped away from his face by flying shrapnel. Instantly he started groaning in pain, the sound blotted out by the rumbling of the moving train. Then he passed out.

The sound of the engine changed, indicating it was slowing for its stop in Kansas City.

"Greg, there is a first-aid kit in the hallway. Quick, get it," Daniel ordered as he started ripping the man's sleeve away from the burned areas.

Greg took only a few seconds to return, handing him a white box with a red cross on it. "What are you going to do?"

"Help me get him into the wheelchair," he said, lifting under one arm and indicating for Greg to lift from the other. "We have got to, Greg. There is no telling when the real porter will find him and how long it will take for him to get to a hospital. Let's help him the best we can."

"Unbelievable," he said sarcastically. "You really ARE unbelievable. Just let him die. Daniel, he tried to kill us!"

"No," Daniel said, opening the kit and removing a bottle of antiseptic and spraying the entire contents onto the burned areas. He then unrolled some sterile bandages and quickly wrapped the man's arm and hand with them. "If we did that, then we become just like him." His hands would not stop shaking while he continued to attend to the burns.

Greg reached in the kit and took out some sticky tape, ripping a piece off with his teeth and giving it to Daniel. There was just enough left on the roll to make it over the guy's cheek, which took the brunt of the explosion. He covered and taped it on the good skin just above and below it. The rest of it they used to wrap each of his arms tightly to the wheelchair, using the last piece to cover his mouth.

"Thank God he passed out," Daniel said. "Look … as soon as the train comes to a stop, we need to get off and start running. There is no telling if he was alone and we can't take a chance. We need to stick together and let's hope Chuck is right out front when we get there," Daniel said, still visibly trembling and his voice quavering. "Look for a limo and run toward it. Keep next to me, Greg. You got it?"

"Got it."

As soon as the train had slowed to almost a stop, they slid open the main railway carriage door and leaped onto the railway station. They both looked in all directions trying to decide where to run, then Greg grabbed Daniel by the arm and pulled him. They began racing to the exit, but as soon as they entered the terminal, Greg spotted the man he had seen twice before. "Run faster, Daniel! Don't slow down for anything!" he yelled.

They burst through both of the terminal entrance doors at once and looked for the limo. "It's not here, it's not here," Daniel repeated in terror.

At that moment, he saw a car speeding toward them blinking its lights. "Greg, it's a Chevy Malibu. Keep running!"

The driver rolled down the side window and Daniel recognized Chuck's voice. "Get in," he said, slowing down and nervously jolting the car to a stop. It started causing the automobile to shutter and almost turn off. The guys fumbled into the back seat, falling on top of each other, before slamming the door shut as the car burst forward.

"Go, go, go!" Daniel hollered as the car started racing off toward the interstate. "Where are we going, Chuck?"

"Our plane is at the downtown airport. Sandy is there waiting for us. What have you gotten yourselves into?" Chuck said, with a blanket of fear now rolling onto him.

"Chuck, I'll tell you when we get to the plane. I'm sorry to bring you into this because these guys are bad … real bad," he repeated.

Chuck fumbled with his cell phone and got Sandy on the line. As soon as she picked up, he started hollering at her. "Tell the pilot to start the engines now and get clearance for take-off! He needs to be ready as soon as we get there. It should be in about ten minutes, maybe less. I gotta go, Sandy. You gotta make this happen, sweetheart."

Daniel and Greg stayed down and out of sight in the back seat while Chuck drove to the Charles B. Wheeler Downtown Airport, observing all of the vehicular laws so as to not attract attention. As soon as they arrived, Chuck pulled directly beside the Gulfstream G280 business jet. The engines were revving as the three men rushed up the steps, locking the cabin hatch behind them and scrambling to a seat.

Sandy was already buckled in, and as soon as the last one clicked shut the plane began to taxi. As the plane turned onto the active takeoff runway, the pilot increased the power. The jet gracefully slid into the air and was soon up and out of sight.

They reiterated the story to them as they had done already so many times along the way. Although they found it hard to accept and not wanting to, they did believe it because of who was telling the story.

Sandy was the first one to speak. "You two have certainly been through a lot. You must have been terrified."

"I can't even begin to tell you how nightmarish it has been. I don't think without my faith that it would have been possible," Daniel said.

"That is why we are here," Chuck said as Sandy nodded her head in agreement.

"What do you mean?" asked Greg.

"I don't know if you know this or not, but Sandy and I are Jewish and share your deep faith in God. Our people have been persecuted throughout history, and many times the Lord has stepped in with miraculous answers to their problems."

"That is exactly what we have been witnessing," Greg said with a twinge of excitement in his voice. "I mean it. Daniel and I would see things happening as if there were angels behind the scenes helping us through it all."

Chuck and Daniel smiled at Greg as Sandy reached out her hand to touch his arm. "*Baruch Hashem Adonai.*" She said the words in Hebrew and repeated the English translation, *"Blessed Be The Name of The Lord.* Chuck and I are here because we believed the Lord wanted us to be here."

"But knowing what Sloan told you, weren't you scared?" Greg asked.

"Of course," Chuck answered, "but you can be scared and still have faith. Courage is moving forward when every fiber of your body is screaming not to. Faith is running headlong into the battle with no thoughts for your own safety, holding onto the expectation that the Lord will defend and protect you."

"I am glad you said that, Chuck," Daniel said. "I have been so scared and thinking that I really shouldn't be. The only thing I could do was be in constant prayer during all of it."

"Well, I doubt that in the beginning King David wasn't scared. But then again he was a different person in a different situation. I think we all have to learn the confidence in our Lord and then I think the time will follow that one can walk into the midst of the battle with a total peace without any doubt that you will be protected. We can only imagine what the Lord has in store for you if He has allowed you to go through all this…. Well, let's not try to figure it all out now. Let's just simply take the time to thank the Lord for being our tower of refuge in times of trouble.[34] You two believe the Messiah has come and we still await Him, but we both believe in the same Lord. May we pray together?"

"Absolutely," Daniel said. "It is always my honor to pray with God's chosen people. I just wish there were more of them that had the depth of faith you two do. You came and got us knowing you were heading into trouble."

All of them got on their knees and worshiped God in their own way, thirty thousand feet above land and clouds while speeding through the air at five hundred miles an hour.

The plane was routed to Bob Hope Airport in Burbank, Ca. After landing they taxied to Atlantic Aviation which catered to many of the private aircraft traveling to and from the Hollywood/Burbank area. They

---

[34] **2 Samuel 22:3** The God of my rock; in him will I trust: he is my shield, and the horn of my salvation, my high tower, and my refuge, my savior; thou savest me from violence.

landed without incident and hoped the rest of the way would not be as harrowing.

The Gulfstream jet pulled next to the hangar and the pilot came into the cabin welcoming them to their destination, which was customary. The whine of the jet became very loud as the pilot unlocked, then pushed the cabin door open and lowered the stairs. Chuck and Sandy were the first to deplane, followed by Daniel and Greg.

As they stood at the top of the steps stunned, both of them began to shiver, the wind whipping their hair from one side to the other. The jet was surrounded by black SUVs ..., all of them with their bright headlights pointed at the plane, clearly awaiting their arrival. The only person they could make out was the one at the bottom of the steps with his gun unholstered ... the one Greg had spotted watching them several times before.

# CHAPTER 22

The engine went silent and they were able to make out his words before he appeared. "What in the world have you two been up to? Are you guys nuts, or is it me?" Special Agent Doug Hensley said, climbing the air-stairs, having walked past the FBI agent guarding the steps. "You two get back into the plane and take a seat. I want to talk to you off the record before we get to interrogation."

"How about Chuck and Sandy?" Greg asked. "Are they going to be okay?"

"Your friends will be fine. We're not even going to give them a citation for the antics they pulled to get you here. Now sit your butts down and tell me why you didn't fly to West Palm Beach as you were supposed to."

Daniel looked at Greg not sure how to answer, finally deciding to just blurt it all out. "Look, when you questioned me, you mentioned you knew about the two guys trying to shove the needle in my arm ... but you couldn't have known that because I never told you about it. You only knew about the guy on the plane to New York."

"Are you two dead from the neck up?" he said, grinning. "I work with the FBI and we work with other agencies. Don't you think I might have found out that you were visiting family in Rome and that your cousin's wife spoke English and that I might have called to speak with her myself? Did you ever stop to think maybe we were trying to help you two, dipsticks?"

Greg looked at Daniel. "We need to go ahead and trust him. He insulted us twice in one sentence. I don't think he would have done that if he really was a bad guy."

"Bad guy ... this gets better and better," he said, chuckling out loud. "After we get done interrogating you, I think our agents are going to want to give you a job with the FBI. No one could believe how you were able to evade us so many times. We were a step behind you because you did so many unexpected things ... and that's saying a lot!"

"Did you get the guy on the train that tried to kill us?" Daniel asked.

"Yes, we have him in custody and I think we will be able to give him some kind of plea deal so he will testify against the ones who hired him. We are working on it. Right now he is in the hospital. My agents tell me the barrel of the gun exploded on the shooter and the doctors told them someone put antiseptic spray on the burns and patched him up before the EMTs arrived. Did you do that?"

"Yes, he was knocked out cold and we had a few minutes before we pulled into Kansas City."

"So you patched up a guy that just tried to kill you?"

"I guess. I don't know," Daniel said, stammering. "We were scared, but it just seemed like the thing to do."

"And how did the gun explode?" Agent Hensley asked.

"Actually, I'm not sure," Daniel admitted.

"I think it may have been because of me," Greg said. "The gun had fallen to the floor and was just out of reach, so I grabbed a pencil and rammed it into the barrel trying to move it closer so I could get it before he did. But it didn't work."

"I get it now and, yes, it did work. In fact, it saved your lives. When you jammed the pencil into the gun, it must have broken, leaving a piece in the barrel. We call that a squib round. It causes the gun to blow up because the bullet can't escape. In this case, it was stuck in the silencer which extends out from the end of the gun. Follow me?"

"Yes," they both said, nodding.

"Anyway, that would have made the explosion about ten times greater than if it didn't have a silencer attached. That guy was lucky it didn't kill him."

Daniel was picturing the moment it happened. "Now that you mention it, I do remember seeing something in the barrel. When he pulled the trigger, the gun was only a few inches from my face." He shuddered thinking about it. "It is a strange thing, but I knew I was about to die and yet my eyes focused on the little piece of wood, or whatever it was … I was looking right at it." Daniel said, amazed. "That is what saved my life?"

"Yes. Evidently, you two must have angels watching out for you or something. In all my years with the FBI, I never heard a story like this one before. Come on, let's go and get you to headquarters. We still have some work to do."

"Wait. We know what we need to do and I don't want you guys to stop us," Daniel said. "This whole thing has been about us protecting the owners of the franchise we work for. Please don't keep us from doing that."

"Well, we can talk it over," Agent Hensley said. "But if we do agree to it, I don't want you two disappearing on me again. You are good guys that are smarter than bad guys and not only able to outsmart the bad guys but also the good guys that are trained to protect you." He shook his head again. "We have had enough of that or I will find something illegal to hold you accountable for and I am sure that will be possible with all you've accomplished. I want to know you guys are hearing me."

"I hear you," Daniel said sheepishly.

"You won't get an argument from me," Greg said. "In fact, do you think I could move into your headquarters until this whole thing blows over?"

"I don't know how the two of you can keep a sense of humor through all this."

"Sense of humor … kidding. Who's kidding? I'm serious," Greg said.

Agent Hensley just looked at him and then turned his gaze toward Daniel, shaking his head. "Go on, get out of here," he said, gesturing toward the exit.

It was daybreak by the time they arrived at the Los Angeles FBI office on Wilshire Boulevard near the 405 Freeway. They spent most of the day in their interrogation room and then, rather than going to a hotel, the agents offered a place where they could get some needed rest, giving Greg his wish.

They spoke to Sloan and everything was worked out with the FBI for their arrival at POP's corporate headquarters the following morning. Originally, when he learned the plane was landing in Burbank, Daniel thought he would go to Dana's nearby, but then realized how little he had thought about her during the past few days. This was the absolute worst time of his life and she had not even been a comforting thought. The truth was he hadn't called her yet and she had no idea he was in Los Angeles.

Greg asked him why and he didn't have an answer. He then offered to talk with him about it when they were finished with their official interrogation. Daniel decided to take him up on it at dinner.

"Here is the basic question, Daniel. Do you love her?"

"Yes, of course, I do, but I am not sure it is the right kind of love. I love her as a friend, but truthfully, I am not 'in love' with her."

"Does she know that?"

Yes, I've always been totally honest with her. In fact, I love her right now, but maybe it is just not the marriage kind of love. She kept telling me that love was a decision and I decided to make that choice. But …"

"But what?"

"But while I was going through all this, I hardly even thought of her. It is like something was missing and … I don't know, like I should have been thinking of her the entire time … but I didn't."

"Well then, maybe in some odd way, all that you went through has helped you make a resolution that was hard to see and face. This is a conversation you need to have with her, Daniel. Right now we need to get ready for tomorrow. Are you ready to deal with it?"

"I think I am," he said, leaning back in his chair. "I never thought we would be having the FBI as back-up. I guess that's a good thing, but from what they tell me, they do not think it is going to help the franchise owners much. They will have to duke that part out on their own." Daniel paused again. "Greg, do you think all we went through is going to be worth it? I mean, do you think it has helped them by us doing what we did, or has it hurt them?"

"Well, I think we have told the truth. Do you have a good conscience before God?"

"Yes, I believe I do. But, Greg, after all we went through, it could end up doing exactly what those greedy reprobates wanted to do in the first place. They could get away scot-free and make a lot of money."

"True, but all we can do is trust God for the outcome. The story won't be finished tomorrow by any means. It'll just be starting. And hey, look at what you got out of the whole thing.… *Me* …" he said with both of his hands pointing to himself, "a new believer."

"Yeah, Greg, I know. I already apologized to God for that. I think overall He's happy about it." He paused, scrunching up his face and pretending that he hated to say what followed. "I use the word 'overall' because I think He is a little concerned that you are in sales, and maybe because of the way you were ogling those girls like you did when we were in Pittsburgh. I mean, it wasn't what you said, but the way you said it." Daniel tried to imitate his words: "Ah, chiquita … very nice … bonita!" Then he added, "Oh, and the clicking sound you did with your voice. PRICELESS!!!"

"Maybe we can take it on the road, Daniel. What do you think?"

"I think we will never forget this, but right now, I think we got to get through tomorrow."

# Chapter 23

The FBI agreed to hang back as Daniel and Greg entered the build-ing, but would be watching them closely to make sure they would remain safe.

Sloan was given the word to send out the email to the owners at exactly 11:11 a.m. It was exactly eleven now.

Mari Lee, POP's Internet Technology Director, was sitting in her wheelchair talking with Susan Heart at the reception desk as they entered.

"Hey, Lickety Split, have you been behaving yourself?" Daniel said to his good friend.

Instantly recognizing his voice, Mari Lee swung her chair around as she powered toward him in high-speed mode. "Daniel, what are you doing here? I have been so concerned because you haven't called me." She stopped her chair about two inches from his toes. "Bend over here and give me a hug," she demanded.

"How can I resist that charm, you bossy, brassy broad you?" he said, giving her a hug.

"And you got that sexy salesman with you. Hi, Greg."

"Do I get a hug, too?" he asked.

"Get over here. You're not escaping me this time," she said.

"This time?" Greg asked.

"Yes, I've been trying to figure out a way to give you a hug for months." Greg leaned over to give her an embrace. She grabbed him by the tie, holding him down. He started to rise up, but she pulled him back. "Hey, where do you think you're going?" She continued talking to Greg while he was bent over in an uncomfortable position. "Look, I hear you go jogging in the park across the street before lunch. How about I meet you and I can ride alongside while you run? My chair goes six miles an hour and I'll keep up, I promise."

"Mari Lee, let him go." Daniel laughed, rolling his eyes. "This is not the time."

"Why?" she said to Daniel. "Greg can jog and then afterward you can join us and we can go to lunch. What do you say, guys?" She reluctantly released her grip on Greg. He stood up with her hand still holding on to his arm.

"Mari Lee, you are relentless," he said, giving her a second hug. "Greg, you might as well say yes and I will join you for lunch. She's harmless and if you don't say yes, she won't let us go."

"Okay, Mari Lee, I'll jog and you talk. I gather talking won't be a problem for you?" he said, smiling at her. "You are a hoot, you know that?"

"I do like that Spanish machismo, Greg, but don't worry, you're safe. I know I'm not marriage material. I just like being seen with good-looking men. It's great for my image."

"I'm not concerned about that. My sister is in a wheelchair and a quirky gaggle of giggles just like you."

"You have a sister in a wheelchair?" asked Daniel.

Greg nodded. "How do you think I could push you around Chicago so easily? I've had plenty of practice."

Hearing familiar voices, Joe Farrow, Director of Operations, stepped into the reception area. They all watched as his eyes practically popped out of his head and began to lose control.

"What are you two doing here?" he demanded in a loud and visibly stunned voice, then quickly disappeared back into the open workspace on the other side of the partition that was surrounded by the executive offices. "Tim! Tim!" he hollered to the President, who was at his desk behind a glass wall and visible to all the employees sitting in their cubicles.

Tim Morrison directed his attention away from the telephone and onto Joe Farrow who was waving his arms into the air to get his attention. He immediately hung up the phone on the person he was speaking with and rushed out of his office to see what the problem was. All of the employees' eyes were on him just as Daniel and Greg made their way around the corner and into the room. Seeing the two of them, he roared with a shocked and terrified tone of voice, "WHAT ARE YOU TWO DOING *HERE?*"

Daniel and Greg, now standing in the midst of the employees who were on their feet in their cubicles, watched as Mack Costello, Daniel's boss, hearing the commotion, entered the room at the same time as Ray Shaman, VP of Sales, and Melinda, Tim's secretary, who had been in the break room.

When Melinda saw them, she lost her normally composed air of authority, bringing her hands up to her face, her eyes widened in fear as she realized the implication of seeing them standing in the office, alive, at the same time as her unscrupulous associates did.

Tim yelled to Mack. "Take Daniel out of here now! Take him into your office. NOW! Ray, you take Greg into yours. Joe, come into my office right now. You hear me? Right now!"

Mack nodded to Daniel for him to follow into his office, and he acknowledged the gesture.

Daniel was awed as he watched the senior staff react in panicked confusion. It was an unusual sensation to know that he was literally standing in the midst of his enemies while at the same time experiencing a complete and total peace ...[35] God, their protector, had visibly turned the very fear and terror that he and Greg went through upon the ones who had

---

[35] **Psalm 23:1–6** The Lord is my shepherd; I shall not want. He maketh me to lie down in green pastures: he leadeth me beside the still waters. He restoreth my soul: he leadeth me in the paths of righteousness for his name's sake. Yea, though I walk through the valley of the shadow of death, I will fear no evil: for thou art with me; thy rod and thy staff they comfort me. Thou preparest a table before me in the presence of mine enemies: thou anointest my head with oil; my cup runneth over. Surely goodness and mercy shall follow me all the days of my life: and I will dwell in the house of the Lord forever.

inflicted it. At that moment, he thought how much he loved the Holy Trinity: Father God, His Son Jesus Christ and the Marvelous Holy Spirit.

"Daniel," Mack said. "What are you doing here?"

"I wanted to deliver a message to you personally … but first, I noticed that you and the senior staff are having a bit of a negative reaction to Greg and I being here in the office. I can't help but wonder what that is all about."

"Daniel …" Mack started to talk when he was interrupted.

"Could it be that you all have become aware that Greg and I have hidden a number of recordings of you and the other senior staff members having private conversations?"

"Daniel …" Mack was visibly shaken now and his hands began trembling.

"Or could it be that you are embarrassed for the amount of times that you tried to kill Greg and I and failed? That must be it, isn't it, Mack?"

Mack, visibly shaken, responded with a very telling answer. "Daniel, I have a small daughter. You met her, remember?"

"Yes, I do. But Mack, you should have thought more of her before you got yourself involved in something like this. By the way, you certainly do have a nice home. It must be sad knowing that you will be in jail and not be able to enjoy the vegetable garden you were going to plant. And your wife, nice lady, I might add. Does she know the truth about you or is this all going to be a big shock to her?"

Telephones started ringing on most everyone's desk as franchise owners began reacting to the email they just received. "How about that? Right on time, 11:11 a.m. That must be the owners calling to let you know they have seen the prospectus with the incredibly embarrassing information about all of you having worked for companies that went into bankruptcy. Gee, Mack, I can only wonder what that is going to do for your reputation."

"Daniel, you son…" He was interrupted by the sound of more commotion going on in the open workspace just out of sight.

The FBI, having monitored everything very closely through hidden body cams mounted on the front and back of Greg and Daniel's clothing, came storming into the workplace with guns raised. They both could hear the agents shouting instructions to everyone, but at that moment were still out of sight.

"Oops, sorry for the distraction, Mack. You were about to say?"

"You are going to pay for this, Daniel."

"Do you mean to tell me that you are willing to risk me giving my secret insurance policy to the FBI?"

"The recordings you mentioned?"

"Exactly, those recordings! Mack, if anything unusual happens to Greg or myself, they will be given to all the powers that matter to you. I am guessing those powers have long enough arms to even reach into prison. Are we clear, Mack?"

"Yes," an expression of pleading in his eyes.

Unknown to Mack, the agents listening were waiting until Daniel mentioned the recordings before giving the okay for the agents to barge in on them. Within a second, one agent was standing at the door with a gun pointed at Mack.

"Oh, and Mack, I forgot to mention the reason I stopped by … I quit."

At the beginning of the siege, Tim Morrison had come out of his office trying to regain a sense of composure, but before he could get a word out of his mouth, Special Agent Doug Hensley started addressing him.

"Tim Morrison, President of POP's Office Supply Franchise, I am placing you under arrest for the attempted murder of Daniel Davidson and Greg Martinez. At this same time my other agents are arresting Joe Farrow, VP, Director of Operations; Mack Costello, VP Marketing; Ray Shaman, Vice President of Sales; Haman Estes, Vice President of Finance; and Executive Secretary Melinda Carlson. They will each be questioned and, if found complicit, will be charged accordingly."

Two of the agents had grabbed each of his arms and handcuffed him. Special Agent Doug Hensley then instructed the employees to leave their desks and to exit the building immediately to an enclosed area of the parking lot.

Tim had been standing a few feet in front of Mari Lee and the agents had squeezed into the space between the two of them. She addressed the agents after Tim had been handcuffed while looking down at the floor and excused herself. "Be careful of your feet agents," Mari Lee warned. "This chair is over three hundred and fifty pounds and I don't want to run over your toes. I'm backing up now."

Moments later Tim Morrison screeched in pain as her wheel made its way over his foot. "Oh," she said, "excuse me. I am usually so careful with my chair around people. It must be all this confusion. Agents, I am so sorry, I was just trying to follow the instructions to leave." At that she wheeled around, spotting the person she was looking for. "Hey, Greg, are you leaving now or do you have to wait?" She paused. "Never mind, I know the answer," she said, turning her chair and filing out of the building behind the other employees.

After the personnel had exited, the senior staff was led out of the building. Leading them was Tim Morrison accompanied by Special Agent Doug Hensley. Each of the others followed in handcuffs, walking next to their own assigned special FBI agent and surrounded by local police. The employees watched as they were loaded into a police van.

Unknown to Daniel and Greg, POP's rumor mill had begun working once the franchise association members leaked information to their favorite employees. By the time the employees saw the senior staff being carted away, most of them could guess why and they began cheering. Some of them took videos on their smartphone that were certain to be available on YouTube by the end of the day. At least if Mari Lee and her team of computer geeks could gather all the videos together quickly enough.

The workforce watched with mixed emotions as the police van pulled out of the parking lot. Each one wondering what exactly would be happening with their jobs and if they would be working there the following day … but at the moment, they were in a celebratory frame of mind.

Their attention then turned to Daniel and Greg as they joined Special Agent Doug Hensley. The entire workforce started clapping in unison, first slowly and then increasing in sound and tempo, before breaking into applause complete with hoot calls and shouts of approval.

# CHAPTER 24

**666**

"Ruination and Furor, take a victory lap in front of all your subordinates, you deserve it," Lucifer said. "You two are named well. Daniel and Greg think they have had a victory, but the only thing they succeeded in doing was persecuting the humans that already belonged to us. Some victory, huh, guys?" He laughed and the sound reverberated in the enclosed area in which they all dwelled. "The franchise shall collapse and with it all 2,000 owners will be groveling at our feet when they run out of money. We will take them once they begin to complain and own them once they give into hate. Shallow victory. We shall be sly and patient, and each of them will come groveling at our feet and not even know they have removed themselves from the protection of the person who calls Himself Supreme and Sovereign."

## 777

"Haszik, will you look at that? The enemy is taking a victory lap when he doesn't even know how much he has lost. His problem has always been his pride and he will live through eternity in Hell."[36]

"What will happen to the franchise owners, Melchior? Some of them have lost everything."

"No, Haszik, they have not lost everything. They have just ended one chapter of their life. How the next chapter turns out will be up to them and will depend completely on how they come through this one. Some will accept it as something that has been put on their plate and deal with it, and hopefully after looking to our Savior, will be drawn closer to Him. Some will give into depressing spirits which will allow the enemy to draw them closer, and then there are the ones that ask for help but only want it their own way. They are the stubborn ones and will

---

[36] **Revelation 20:1-3** And I saw an angel come down from heaven, having the key of the bottomless pit and a great chain in his hand. And he laid hold on the dragon, that old serpent, which is the Devil, and Satan, and bound him a thousand years, And cast him into the bottomless pit, and shut him up, and set a seal upon him, that he should deceive the nations no more, till the thousand years should be fulfilled: and after that he must be loosed a little season.
**Matthew 8:12** But the children of the kingdom shall be cast out into outer darkness: there shall be weeping and gnashing of teeth.

remain as they already were and will spend an eternity with the enemy anyway. Unless, of course, they repent. That is always an option to every human as long as they are breathing. To all those that ask for the Lord's help, they shall receive it."[37]

"How is that?"

"Well, their prayers may not be answered exactly as they were asked, because many of them will ask for things that will lead them away from God. He would never allow that because He loves them too much. Our Lord will only answer those prayers that will lead a soul closer to Him and give them the opportunity to know Him in a personal way.[38]

"I love that about our God. I have seen Him often leave a human crying, not because He doesn't love them but because, like any parent, He knows what is best for His child, and when a parent knows what is best they have compassion for the tears yet strength to know what they are doing is best for the child."

"So what do we do now?" Haszik asked.

"Watch and wait," Melchior said, folding his hand and looking upwards. "The decisions have to be their own, both good and bad ones, but," he said, smiling, "if they pray, we are allowed to point them in the right direction."

"I think Daniel and Greg are very resourceful humans … they really do want to help their franchise owners," Haszik said.

"I agree." Melchior began to sit down on a rock which instantly appeared beneath him. "Let us rest a moment. To us time is nothing but a flit, a breath, a vapor.[39] We will check back in three years of their time

---

[37] **Matthew 7: 8** For every one that asketh receiveth; and he that seeketh findeth; and to him that knocketh it shall be opened.

[38] **John 17:3** And this is life eternal, that they might know thee the only true God, and Jesus Christ, whom thou hast sent.
**Philippians 3:8** Yea doubtless, and I count all things but loss for the excellency of the knowledge of Christ Jesus my Lord: for whom I have suffered the loss of all things, and do count them but dung, that I may win Christ.

[39] **2 Peter 3:8** But, beloved, be not ignorant of this one thing, that one day is with the Lord as a thousand years, and a thousand years as one day.

to see what has happened." Then as quickly as he sat down to rest, he stood again recharged. "Now we have pressing matters to attend to. There is someone reading a story about God and believes in us and they have deeply prayed in faith for His help. A few of them have even entered their own dark night of the soul like Daniel did. So let's go, angel that I love. We have work to do."

*****

James 4:14 Whereas ye know not what shall be on the morrow. For what is your life? It is even a vapor, that appeareth for a little time, and then vanisheth away.

# Epilogue

"**L**adies and gentlemen, please take your seats," Daniel said as he watched the crowd cease from conversations. "You are the remnant." He paused, looking around the group of almost seven hundred people. "A little more than three years ago, you became like David standing strong against Goliath. The victorious class action suit has allowed all of you to continue your own businesses with merely a name change. About one-third of the owners left franchising behind, another third chose to remain with the original POP's franchise and we wish every one of them much success. But you people … you are the ones who join us in our faith in both God and our franchise. You could have left without ever paying any business fees again, but you renewed your obligation and chose to come under this new umbrella, to have a new identity.

"The last time we met, it was right here in Atlantic City. The only difference is that we had more people than we do now. At the time, we all had great hopes for our future … then we hit a bump in the road." Daniel waited as the audience mumbled. "Okay," he said, "so maybe it was more like a major pothole." He listened as the audience continued to talk between themselves, recalling their own painful and regrettable memories. "But now we start out again … a new beginning at a new Conclave. But we could not be here if it weren't for the actions of our next well-loved and 'illustrious' franchise owner." Daniel emphasized the word as he waved for her to join him. As she began to climb the steps to the podium, the applause continued until Daniel interrupted.

"Well, my friend, the last time we saw you, I think we would agree that you were having a bad day." Daniel put his arm around her shoulders and gave her a hug while he addressed the audience. "How many of you hope that in the future the only days she will have will be her own kind of good days? You know … her own, Dottie Dayes!" The owners started applauding and stood to their feet, many having heard the rumors that had circulated about the incident surrounding it and applauding her courage.

"Thank you, Daniel, and all of you. It is good to see everyone again." She paused. "Both here in Atlantic City and actually," she continued with a smile, "I might add, amongst the living." The applause got louder. "I guess our work here on earth is not done yet."

Daniel reached on the chair behind him and turned to the audience. "I think most of you know this, but for those who don't, Dottie was the first who began to suspect that something was amiss with the senior staff. She sounded the alarm arranging the meeting with Greg and myself at the last Conclave. Dottie is here with us, but several others who were at that meeting were not so fortunate. Sadly, they passed away upon returning from the convention. We will speak more of them at our dinner tonight, but now is a time for celebration, a time we are all together again."

Daniel unwrapped the plaque he was holding. "I think you know how hard it was to come up with our new franchise name, but in the end there was only one name that carried most of the vote. *POP POP's Office Supply.*" Daniel waited until the applause died down. "With great appreciation to Dottie for all she has done, we want to present her with this plaque … I hope," he paused, "she won't mind the name we chose for her. We wanted to come up with a name for a person who looks out for others. We considered the titles caregiver, au pair, governess, but in the end decided on one with a bit more levity. Starting this year, in the name of Winnie LaTrove who is no longer with us, we will be presenting this award to the most deserving franchise owner at Conclave. Dottie, we present you with the POP POP's NANNY award." The audience laughed in approval. "So, Dottie, if Winnie LaTrove was still with us, she would be presenting this award and I am sure she would have had something better to say than me. But from all of us … a heart-felt thank-you."

Dottie accepted it, laughing with the rest of the crowd. "Nanny, Daniel … really, you are calling me a nanny?" she said, trying to conceal a laugh. "I think you might be cruising for a bruising. We're going to have to have a serious conversation after the meeting." Dottie lifted up the plaque for the audience to see. "I accept this as a gift from Winnie LaTrove, and knowing her, she probably had something to do with calling me a nanny, just to get my goat!" she said lovingly about her friend. The crowd applauded as she made her way back to her seat.

"Oh, and Dottie, please take your seat quietly this time … no drama, okay?" Daniel said, teasing.

"I'll try real hard," she quipped while waving to the audience before taking her seat.

Daniel continued. "Greg and I have both been humbled. Greg, would you please join me now?" Greg, who had been sitting next to his wife Mari Lee, who held their infant daughter Faith in her lap, stood up holding her twin brother and scaled the three steps up to the podium.

"What, you need help already?" he said when he arrived. Almost everyone in the room began to laugh, remembering the unforgettable moment Winnie made fun of Will at the Conclave several years before. The nostalgic moment seemed to carry on for more than a minute as some owners broke into tears.

"Okay, smart-aleck. What would you like to say?"

"First, that I said those words in fond memory of Winnie LaTrove, who is sorely missed by all of us who knew her. She was a special person." He paused as the audience stood applauding and turning toward Will who was sitting in the first row. "Secondly, we want to thank Will LaTrove for funding this new business venture. We are here because he used his own finances to continue the legacy that he and Winnie began. We all thank him."

"Now are you done?" Daniel asked, nudging him away from the microphone. "If you don't mind, we must get to some serious work."

"What, are you saying what I was doing was not serious?" Greg said, teasing.

Daniel removed the mic from its holder and turned to the audience and lowered his voice. "Don't tell anyone, but it is hard for me to take anything he says seriously … He's in sales, you know!" The crowd began laughing as Will LaTrove walked up the steps to join them on the podium as the applause skyrocketed.

"Hey, Greg, we better behave ourselves now. Here comes Pop Pop."

"Fat chance that will happen with you, Daniel," Will said, laughing. "I know you too well. Okay, you two. Can you believe these two gentlemen are the president and vice president of POP POP's Office Supply Franchise?" At that Greg and Daniel took their place on either side of Will as he continued. "If I am Pop Pop, what does that make the two of you?"

Daniel reached over and pulled the mic in front of himself. "Very fortunate." The crowd responded with applause.

Greg leaned into the mic. "I'll second that." Then added, "Daniel, is it true what we heard about Will?"

"What have you heard, Greg?"

"I heard that Will is now president of the B'nai B'rith organization." Greg pulled some notes out of his suit pocket. "B'nai B'rith's mission is to unite persons of the Jewish faith and to enhance their identity on behalf of Jewish people throughout the world. In recent years, the organization reported hundreds of thousands of members and supporters in countries around the world with a budget of $14,000,000."

"So you are saying it is big and he is their president?" Daniel asked again. "Does that mean he got a promotion?"

"I am saying that I think he is a Jewish man who believes in God," Greg said.

"I agree. I think all that we have to do is look at the way he ran this franchise, with transparency, honesty and integrity." The crowd broke out in applause and stood to their feet again.

"He sounds like a man we can turn to if we need help. In fact, many of us did just that!" The crowd applauded again. "Hey, I have an idea, Greg. Since this is the first time all of us have come together, how about we ask him to lead us in prayer? The Jewish people are still waiting for the arrival of the Messiah while we Christians believe Jesus has already come …, but we both worship Father God. And if any of the owners wish to join us, they can commit *our franchise* and their own locations to the Lord. Is there anyone here that would like to do that?"

Everyone in the room began to stand until they were all on their feet.

Will addressed the audience. "It would be my privilege to say a prayer in Hebrew, and Daniel, afterward I think it would be a blessing for you to lead the Christian prayer as the new president of POP POP's Office Supply."

"Of course. Thank you for the privilege."

Will began his prayer in Hebrew and Daniel followed, after which many of the owners repeated the Lord's prayer in unison. Some of them were bowing their heads and some were kneeling in front of their seats.

Greg cradled his son while holding the baby in a position so the audience could watch him waving his arms and chewing on the edge of his toy. Sounding like punctuation to the end of the prayer, Joshua started cooing loudly with a happy giggle and then reached his tiny fingers toward the microphone while shaking his pacifier. The tinkling sound of its bells resonated through all of the speakers in the large conference room, bringing a smile to everyone's face.

Haszik and Melchior invisibly kissed Joshua on the head before dematerializing … for the moment at least.

End

*…and your beginning?*

# Author's Note

You have just read the story of Daniel who heard so vividly from the Lord during his time of personal crisis. The Bible is very clear that each and every one of us can have our own relationship with the Lord Jesus Christ. This promise <u>absolutely includes you!</u> I wish, as the author, I could hear so clearly all the time, but I have learned there are many voices that fight to get to the forefront of our minds. They might include our own will or desire for a certain outcome, or someone's advice that repeats in our thoughts. Just be careful as, in many cases, our true enemy, Satan and his demons, will imitate the voice of the Lord sometimes closely … but they are instead false. I caution you to be careful of the voice you follow.

The Bible commands that in order to know Him personally, there must first be repentance, or a turning away from sin. It may not disappear immediately, but there must be a sincere effort and a pursuing of the Lord for His help in your own individual circumstances.

Below are a few Bible verses to help get you started. If you are serious about getting to know Him in your own unique way, you must begin to read the Bible. The first line in the Gospel of John says, "In the beginning was the Word, and the Word was with God, **and the Word was God**." Wow, the Bible is literally God's own Words to us.

I wish you well on your own personal journey. I can guarantee you that it may not be an easy road, but I am POSITIVE you will discover that He is an awesome God.

**John 10:27** - My sheep hear my voice, and I know them, and they follow me.

**John 14:26** - But the Comforter, which is the Holy Ghost, whom the Father will send in my name, he shall teach you all things, and bring all things to your remembrance, whatsoever I have said unto you.

**Acts 3:19** - Repent ye therefore, and be converted, that your sins may be blotted out, when the times of refreshing shall come from the presence of the Lord.

**Matthew 10:30** - But the very hairs of your head are all numbered.

**Luke 10:27** - And he answering said, Thou shalt love the Lord thy God with all thy heart, and with all thy soul, and with all thy strength, and with all thy mind; and thy neighbor as thyself.

**Mark 12:30** - And thou shalt love the Lord thy God with all thy heart, and with all thy soul, and with all thy mind, and with all thy strength: this is the first commandment.

**Revelation 3:19–21** – As many as I love, I rebuke and chasten: be zealous therefore, and repent. Behold, I stand at the door, and knock: if any man hear my voice, and open the door, I will come in to him, and will sup with him, and he with me. To him that overcometh will I grant to sit with me in my throne, even as I also overcame, and am set down with my Father in his throne.

# Peppino
## A Nineteenth Century Medici

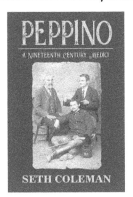

*Kirkus Review:* *A fast-moving historical tale of religious and class conflicts. Coleman…jumps quickly from one action packed event to another in fast-paced storytelling that's highly enjoyable.*

Loosely bathis historical novel tells the tale of Peppino, an upper- class trouble-maker in a small Italian village who resents the restrictions of his highborn status and longs to fight for the common people.

In late-19th-century Italy, the village of Brancaleone is divided by an imaginary line that keeps the poor from fraternizing with the rich. Teenage Peppino resents this division, which prevents him, a baroness' son, from being able to freely socialize with his peasant friend Emilio. He also resents the monsignor, the local head of the church; more corrupt than godly, he uses his position of power to manipulate the locals for his own gain. When Emilio enlists Peppino to help rescue local hero Nicola from being executed, Pep- pino finds his life finally veering off the narrow, upper-class path previously laid out for him. From fraternizing with outlaws, a stint at a monastery, being accused of murder and meeting Pope Leo XIII, Peppino's journey leads to much personal growth—and a few startling revelations. … Peppino's conversations with a Hasidic Jew named Abramo provide interesting insight into the era's attitudes toward religion. Coleman (*Critical Transfer*, 2013), who based the novel on his grandfather's exploits, jumps quickly from one action-packed event to another in fast-paced storytelling that's highly enjoyable. Despite Peppino's fascinating interactions, the baroness proves to be the most compelling character. Her complex relationship with Peppino and the mixture of love and resentment they seem to share are more intriguing than many of Peppino's exchanges with the more heroic characters of the story.

# Critical Transfer

*Kirkus Review*: *"Coleman's characters are vivid and believable...(W)ell-drawn locations and intriguing characters keep this thriller enjoyable."*

When American computer executive Peter Barrett's multi-million dollar business deal backfires, his life is turned upside down as he becomes the most hunted man in the United States. He is accused of embezzling money from his father-in-law's firm to be used by terrorists intending to fire missiles at South Florida and major cities on the East Coast. With the help of an old friend, he manages to outsmart the FBI, the CIA, the local police in California and Florida, and the entire government of Fidel Castro as he tries to smuggle himself into and then out of Cuba...but not without a lot of close calls. From an upper-class businessman to a wanted criminal and eventually to a modern-day hero the American public is rooting for, Peter must risk everything to prove his innocence and get his life back.

Critical Transfer is an exhilarating new thriller about a man attempting to accomplish the impossible while facing incredible odds. An adrenaline-charged pace combined with gripping suspense make this exciting novel a must-read for fiction fans around the world. By expertly traversing topics of love, devotion, revenge, and terrorism, this enthralling story by Seth Coleman will captivate readers from the opening page and won't let go until the final words have been read.

With Cuba as an antagonist, Critical Transfer crafts a truly unique story with the use of an enemy that is dangerously close to home. An integrated blend of action, adventure, and suspense, this compelling novel will fascinate readers from all backgrounds and keep readers leaping from one chapter to the next.